Feb. 1973

I suggest you read the Epilogue p.199 and the two following essays before starting novel.

B.M.S.

BLACKSTONE

BLACKSTONE marks the debut of Edmund Blackstone, Bow Street Runner, whose adventures and cases will form a vivid and exciting series of novels. In Blackstone's time, around the 1820s, the Bow Street Runners were at the height of their fame, but beginning to come under pressure from Sir Robert Peel, Home Secretary and founder of the Metropolitan Police.

This first novel of the series concerns a kidnap attempt on the young Princess Victoria, whom Blackstone has been ordered to guard.

BLACKSTONE

Richard Falkirk

LONDON
EYRE METHUEN
1972

First published 1972
Copyright © 1972 Richard Falkirk
Printed in Great Britain for
Eyre Methuen
11 New Fetter Lane, London EC4P 4EE
by Ebenezer Baylis and Son Limited
The Trinity Press, Worcester and London

SBN 413 44940 8

PART ONE

Chapter One

⁂

THE black carriage waited at the roadside, its whippy lines deliberately disguised by mud and shabbiness, its racing horses temporarily replaced by bowed pensioners. Inside two men waited, one with paper and pencil, the other with a watch. Between them on the leather seat, which was in far better condition than the coachwork, lay two pocket pistols.

The man with the paper spoke. 'I'm coming with you this time.' He had a quiet voice edged with London corners – The Dials, the 'dolly' shops, the gin shops – but not too sharp, as if its owner had tried to round them. His face was not quite as ruthless as the duelling scar from eye to mouth seemed to make it. His name was William Challoner; Mister to most, Bill to those for whom the scar occasionally smiled, but they were few, very few. He was forty, looked thirty-five, and there were many more scars on his body.

His companion, Harry Malt, aged twenty-five, feebly handsome and smart in his Charles Macintosh waterproofed coat, said: 'I shouldn't bother, Bill.'

Challoner stuck a pistol in his belt beneath his coat. 'I didn't know we were on such familiar terms, Malt.'

'All right, Mister Challoner then.'

Harry Malt was a professional agitator, paid to incite starving country labourers to rebellion with lies and sovereigns. When the Hussars cut down the rebels Harry Malt was far away.

Challoner was an assassin.

'What time is it?'

'Half past three.'

7

'Time to go.' Challoner made a pencilled note.

'You haven't come with me before.'

'So?'

'Don't you trust me to carry out a little job like this?'

Challoner looked at him speculatively. At the rings on his fingers, the imitation breeding on his face. 'No,' he said. And when they were on the road he asked: 'Haven't you forgotten something?'

'My pistol.' Malt retrieved it from the coach and thrust it in his belt. 'You make me like this, as nervous as if I were in front of the beak.'

Challoner said: 'Be quiet, Malt.'

They crossed the road and entered Kensington Gardens. The air smelled of chestnuts and soot and dying chrysanthemums killed that night by the first frost. Along the pathways babies in perambulators cried while their nursemaids with 'Scarlet Fever' flirted with soldiers in red, hungry for food and other comforts in the servants' quarters.

'Here they come,' Malt said. He looked at his watch. 'Three thirty-two. Dead on time. How many more times are we going to go through this performance?'

Challoner made another note. 'This is the last time this week. Once more next week just to make sure they're keeping to their routine.'

Two hundred yards away a group of elegant people sauntered towards them in the brief butterfly sunshine. A mother perpetually worried, a German governess smelling of caraway seeds, a nursemaid, two liveried footmen and a child of six or seven with blue eyes and fair hair in ringlets. An assured child, not quite precocious.

Ten yards behind walked a man carrying a baton. Also elegant but not completely familiar with his elegance. He walked warily like a man surrounded by hidden enemies.

Challoner took Malt's arm, fingers gripping the bicep, and led him into the shadows at the entrance to the Gardens. 'You didn't tell me about him.'

'Tell you about who? What are you talking about, Mr

Challoner?' And as an afterthought: 'You're hurting my arm.'

'The bodyguard.'

'I told you there was a bodyguard. There's bound to be, isn't there. But he doesn't know anything about us.'

'Are you sure, Malt?'

'Of course I'm sure. He'd have done something by now, wouldn't he? Nobody's noticed me yet and I always make myself scarce before they reach the entrance.'

'Do you know who he is, Malt?'

Malt tried unsuccessfully to remove Challoner's hand. 'No, why should I? I can see he's a Bow Street Runner but just because I've been in trouble in the past doesn't mean to say I know them all by name.'

'Villains with authority,' Challoner said. 'A dangerous combination, my covey.'

'So he's a Runner. So what? Some people seem to be scared out of their wits by them.' Malt faltered. 'Not you, of course, Bill – Mr Challoner. But,' he hurried on, 'they're not so special, are they? A load of villains, too, by all accounts.'

'Villains with authority,' Challoner said again. 'A dangerous combination.'

The group was a hundred yards away now. The mother and the governess talking in German. The footmen eyeing other nursemaids abroad this chestnut afternoon – the nursemaids eyeing them back because after the soldiers you had to find security. The little girl skipped and pointed, chattering in German and English, playing with a water dog accompanying the party.

The Bow Street Runner proceeded behind them, authority and wariness sparring with each other in his bearing. He wore a broadcloth greatcoat, a tall grey hat and charcoal grey trousers fastened with straps under the instep. His face had lines of struggle upon it with humorous interludes: a handsome, successful face with traces of uncertainty lingering. The sort of face that Challoner might have possessed if things had been different.

Challoner said: 'Let's get back to the coach.'

9

'I usually stay a little longer to get the timetable completely accurate,' Malt boasted. 'They sometimes stop about there.' He pointed down the pathway. 'In the summer the little bitch used to ride on a donkey. That's not likely now, is it Mr Challoner? I mean it would complicate things, wouldn't it? Too cold now for donkey-riding, I should think,' he added, worry oozing from his pores.

'Too cold to stand around here,' Challoner said. 'What's more I don't want that flash bastard with the baton to see us.'

'Why, do you know him?' Malt was inspired by the furtive intuition that helped him select doomed recipients for inducements in country inns.

'Yes, I know him.'

They walked rapidly out of the Gardens, treading the crisp leaves, reaching the coach just as Her Royal Highness the Duchess of Kent and her daughter, Princess Alexandrina Victoria, heir to the throne of England, reached the point where they had been standing.

Challoner snapped his fingers at the driver. 'Off you go.' He climbed inside with agility, followed by Malt.

As the old horses moved away beneath the whip which they had known all their lives Malt spoke again. But his voice had assumed the tone of a man who has discovered weakness in the hitherto unassailable. A child who has spotted a teacher's vice. 'Are you scared of that Runner, Challoner?'

Challoner looked at him and Malt knew dreadfully that he had made a mistake.

'Scared of him, Malt?'

'A slip of the tongue, Mr Challoner. But you did say you knew him . . . I suppose you just didn't want him to recognize you. That was it, wasn't it, Mr Challoner? You didn't want him to recognize you.'

Challoner didn't reply and Malt thanked God.

The coach swayed past Kensington Palace towards the market gardens of Fulham.

After a while Malt, whose tongue would take him to the gallows, asked: 'Who was that Runner, Mr Challoner?'

'It doesn't matter,' Challoner said.

Five minutes later Malt tried again. 'Did you know him very well?'

'His name,' Challoner said, 'is Blackstone.' He laid his pistol on his knee and leaned forward. 'Now shut your mouth, Malt. I don't want to hear your whining voice again until we reach Fulham.'

And it seemed to Harry Malt, who had never heard of Blackstone, that the name filled the carriage.

Chapter Two

_____

FROM the half-curtained window of the Russian Hotel, better known as the Brown Bear, Edmund Blackstone gazed across the road at Nos 3 and 4 Bow Street, headquarters of the Runners, and wondered whether he should protest by offering his resignation.

At No. 4 in particular. The well-bred building in which he had first signed on for the Foot Patrol and clawed himself out of the past. Where he had been promoted to the plain-clothes Runners and acquired respect from others and himself. Until now.

He drank deeply from his pot of ale and watched George Ruthven, the Runner who had been ahead of them when they raided the Cato Street conspirators, enter the building. October sunshine lent the four-storeyed terrace house with its railinged area a delicacy belied by its history.

That house represents the only security I've ever known, Blackstone thought. Echoing with law and order (who would have thought he would ever respect that?), stern with magisterial ghosts. Henry Fielding who spawned the Runners, John Fielding, the 'Blind Beak' who could recognize three thousand thieves by their voices – so they said.

The magistrate on his dais, clerk below, the jostling throngs of spectators. And at the bar assassins, swindlers, rioters, strumpets, murderers, horse-stealers, skittle sharks and pea-and-thimble riggers, highwaymen, arsonists, footpads, receivers. From bar to sessions to gaol or transportation or gallows.

Blackstone glanced up and down the bow-shaped street

waiting in the thin sunshine for winter when the children exploited by criminals might survive; or they might die. Soon, Blackstone thought, there would be no more rotten plums for the army of 100,000 vagrants to scavenge round the corner in Covent Garden.

He finished his ale and ordered some more. One more pot and a few pennyworth of hot gin and he would resign. Return to the only other way of making a living he knew.

He sipped his beer at the window of the inn at No. 34 managed by a Mr G. Hazard whose sign proclaimed 'Lodgings for Gentlemen'. The sign didn't mention the cell which until recently had served as an extension to No. 4 and had accommodated many who were somewhat less than gentlemen.

Ruthven came in with a Runner called Page and ordered two brandies. 'Proper brandy,' he told the girl. 'Not English brandy made from cider and molasses.'

The girl was surly. 'We'd hardly do that here, opposite No. 4, would we?'

'Nor opposite No. 3,' Ruthven said. 'That's where most of the felons' rooms are.' He gestured to Blackstone. 'And you, Blackie, what are you having?'

'Gin with some hot water,' Blackstone said.

'Don't get too groggy. Birnie says he wants to see you in fifteen minutes.'

'It's me who wants to see him.'

'Don't be so bloody prickly,' Ruthven said. He had a pleasant boxer's face on a gang-busting frame.

Page, whose speciality was pickpockets, said: 'We know how you feel.' A quick darting man was Page, although big and pale.

'You don't know anything of the sort. Birnie didn't pick you.'

'It could have been any of us,' Page said, hands running lightly over his pockets in imitation of his prey.

Blackstone pointed at Ruthven. 'Can you imagine him as a nursemaid?'

Ruthven shrugged. 'Nor you, Blackie.' He tossed back his brandy, the glass a thimble in his hand.

Page caught himself picking his own pocket and said: 'Another, Blackie?'

'Why not?'

The girl put the glasses before them, her breasts very close to Blackstone's face.

Ruthven said: 'Who's looking after Her Royal Highness in your absence?'

'I know who isn't,' Page said. 'I'll wager it isn't Townsend.'

'You're right,' Blackstone said. The knowledge angered him even more. 'He's probably dining with the Duke of Wellington.' He thought: Why me? Why did it have to be me?

'You know,' Ruthven observed, 'you should be honoured. Guarding the future Queen of England. Has it occurred to you that you were specially picked for the job?'

'What makes you think that?'

Ruthven spoke slowly because his hands, not words, were his weapons. 'Because you have bearing.'

'Bearing be damned.' But a tiny glow of pleasure was lit somewhere.

'And you're one of the best men Birnie's got. Ask any cracksman in London. You're a . . .' The dictionary closed in his mind.

'A deterrent,' Page said.

Blackstone permitted himself a smile, angry at the same time that he was so vulnerable to flattery. 'I was picked,' he said, 'as a punishment. We all know that.'

Across the road a day foot patrol passed by. Blue coats and trousers, red waistcoats, black felt hats. One stopped to talk to a girl wearing a poke bonnet and holding a parasol.

'That's what you should be worrying about,' Ruthven said. 'Not the ig . . .'

'Ignominy,' Page supplied.

'. . . not the ignominy of looking after Princess Alexandrina Victoria. They're the bastards who'll have us all out of our jobs soon. Peel and his Redbreasts. Who does he think he's fooling?'

'A lot of people by all accounts,' Blackstone said, happy to redirect his anger. 'Birnie reckons the people will never stand for a uniformed police force. But they will. It'll be swindled through Parliament just like any other law, whether the people want it or not. And *they're* just the beginning' – pointing at the red-chested patrol. 'Peel pretends they're only an enlargement of Bow Street. In fact they're his advance guards. He wants to fill London with his Peelers just like he filled Ireland.'

The girl who had returned with drinks said: 'They look very smart, don't they?' one breast warm on Blackstone's cheek.

Page said: 'Popinjays.'

'Could you see me in a pretty red waistcoat?' Ruthven asked the girl.

'Not really,' the girl said. 'But then I could never imagine Blackie as a nursemaid.' She removed her breast and herself to a safe distance.

'She hears too much, that one,' Ruthven said.

'Don't worry,' Blackstone said. 'She'll keep quiet.'

'You sound very sure of yourself,' Page said.

Blackstone shrugged and took out his gold Breguet watch. 'I'd better be getting over there, I suppose.'

'One more for the road,' Ruthven said. 'Where's everyone else, by the way?'

'There *are* only eight of us,' Page said. 'Townsend's about his own business somewhere. That only leaves four. Wheeler's on duty in the House of Commons. Sayer's at the Bank of England while they pay out the dividends. Handley's on the murder down at Fetcham and Chandler's guarding His Majesty at Windsor, seeing that he doesn't get too drunk and fall in the river or marry Mrs Fitzherbert again or do any stupid thing that comes into his head.'

'Poor old Prinny,' Ruthven remarked.

Page said: 'He should have stayed Prinny and not become King of England. Still,' he conceded, 'he's given *us* some sport in his time.'

'And his wife,' Ruthven added. 'You were on that, Blackie, weren't you?'

Blackstone said he was. Remembering the rioting at Queen Caroline's funeral when arrangements had been made to ship her body from Harwich because she had asked to be buried in Brunswick. But, fearing demonstrations for a popular Queen and against an unpopular King, the Prime Minister, Lord Liverpool, had diverted the procession at Hyde Park. But the mob had got wind of it and stopped the cortège. For one and a half hours the crowd fought until the Bow Street Magistrate, Sir Robert Blake, was forced to call in the Life Guards. But this made the fighting more savage. Blake was sacked and Richard Birnie got the job as chief magistrate and London's unofficial police chief.

'Stirring times,' Ruthven said. 'You became a Runner just at the right moment, Blackie.'

Page said: 'If it wasn't for the Monarchy, God bless 'em, we'd be without jobs. The last king as mad as a hatter. This one a drunken sot. They say he couldn't even speak when he got to Dublin. The next one a good-hearted simpleton who's already lived in sin for twenty years. And the next . . .' he looked at Blackstone, hands fluttering at his waistcoat, '. . . the next one rather depends on you, Blackie.' He sipped at his brandy like a bird pecking. 'What's she like?'

'She's all right,' Blackstone said. 'She'll be a good Queen if she reaches the throne . . .'

'Which she will because Sweet William won't last all that long. Is there any doubt in your mind about her safety, Blackie?'

'No doubt,' Blackstone said.

'You don't sound too sure.'

Ruthven asked: 'What does she think about becoming Queen?'

'She doesn't know,' Blackstone said.

'Poor little girl,' Ruthven said.

Blackstone stood up and stared across at the lighted frame of No. 4 with the smaller No. 3 shouldering it in the terrace. The evening was smoky and cruel: a knifing night, an assassin's night.

'You'll have me in tears soon,' Blackstone said.

'Or Birnie will,' Ruthven told him. 'You're three minutes late. Come back and tell us what happens.'

As he walked out the girl called out: 'Don't forget to change the nappies, Blackie.'

He crossed the street slowly, feeling the cruelty of the evening. Somewhere near the Market a woman was selling 'lily-white vinegar', her cry a plea in the acrid dusk. Somewhere beneath the streets the tosher-men were ending the day's work combing the sewers for valuables. Somewhere in a workhouse the child of a starving mother was being delivered still-born. Smoke and gaslight and sharp stars.

The carriages of the rich trotted by, wheels clattering on the cobblestones. Back to coal fires freshly bellowed, the *Morning Herald*, a glass of whisky, pigeon pie, bed warmed, a glance at the children, nurserymaid overpaid at £7 a year: the hostile night cut off by the closing front door. But some of the privileged will be robbed this night, Blackstone thought. And one or two will have their throats cut.

I'm drunk, he acknowledged, as muddled grievance surfaced. But the muddle is never sorted out, merely quieted, suppressed by work and success and flattery; by a woman's touch, by a bottle of wine. You, Blackstone, should be hunting the robbers, not secretly applauding them because of their victims' birthright, because of inequality.

What is your birthright, Edmund Blackstone?

Waiting outside Birnie's office he wondered if the Magistrate would realize that he was drunk. Most probably. The liquor was a marble beneath his tongue.

Birnie called out: 'Come in, Blackstone.'

Sir Richard Birnie, one-time saddlemaker, sat at his desk, his tough old face charmed a little by the firelight. 'I saw you come out of the Brown Bear, Blackstone.'

The marble rolled beneath his tongue. 'I had a couple of drinks, sir.'

'Drinking,' Birnie observed, 'is hardly suited to your present duties.'

When in 1820 George Ruthven led the assault on the Cato Street Conspirators who were plotting to murder the Cabinet, seize the Bank of England and proclaim a provisional government, the Runners were under Birnie, the Assistant Bow Street Magistrate, sixty years old at the time. Always the bridesmaid never the bride, it seemed – a permanent No. 2.

He had come from Scotland penniless but determined. A saddlemaker who had attracted the attention of the Prince of Wales and married the daughter of a wealthy baker.

Now in 1826 at the age of sixty-five he had fulfilled his ambition. And because of his ordinary beginnings the Runners, and the men on the horse and foot patrols, believed they respected him all the more. Blackstone included. But the respect fostered because he was 'one of them' was, Birnie thought, a debatable quality. Might they not have respected him all the more if he had been a gentleman, a barrister?

Everyone agreed that he was a tough old bastard. And an ally against Robert Peel who had been Secretary of State for the Home Department for three years.

Birnie said: 'I gather you wanted to see me.' He wore black with an old-fashioned collar standing high around his neck, and a black cravat. His moorland face still resented the city to which ambition had brought him.

'It's about my new duties, sir.'

'What about your duties, Blackstone?'

'I don't think they're in accord with the dignity of the Bow Street Runners.'

Birnie lit his churchwarden pipe. 'You speak very well, Blackstone.'

Patronizing, Blackstone thought: we've both taught ourselves to dig the common flints out of our voices.

Birnie went on: 'I think you are mistaken, however. Bodyguard to the future Queen is surely a very important duty. In fact,' he added, injecting a thin jet of smoke into the sooty fumes from the fire, 'you were specially chosen for the job.' He might have smiled; Birnie's smiles were hard to catch.

'Because no one else would have it? And because you wanted

to punish me because I got rough with a flashman living off the immoral earnings of thirteen-year-old girls.'

'The protection of the Monarchy,' Birnie said, 'has been the responsibility of the Runners since 1786 when that mad woman Margaret Nicholson attacked George III. Townsend and Macmanus got the job, then Sayer. There's nothing undignified about it. Chandler's down at the Royal Lodge now guarding the King.'

'Making sure his dirty letters don't get into the wrong hands, I suppose.'

Birnie, who had managed to retain private asceticism despite his daily meeting with bawdy London, ignored him. 'And that's why you're guarding the heir to the throne.'

'I'm guarding her,' Blackstone said, 'because her mother's touched and believes there's a plot to kidnap her. Why does she believe that for God's sake?'

'Calm down,' Birnie warned. 'Don't let the gin talk for you.'

'I'm telling you, sir, she's demented. According to Chandler she even thought the King was going to kidnap the Princess down at Windsor. They all went out in the carriage together – the King, Lady Conyngham, Lord Seward, the Duchess of Kent, the Princess and her half-sister Feodore. The Princess apparently sat on the King's knee and kissed his rouged cheek.'

'I know,' Birnie said. 'I've heard all about it. The King said to her, "Give me your little paw" and afterwards Lady Conyngham pinned the King's miniature on her dress.' Birnie didn't seem to find any of it very touching.

'Then next day the Princess was given another ride by the King – and the Duchess of Kent promptly imagines that he's going to kidnap her. Why, for God's sake?'

'She *is* German,' Birnie observed, as if that explained everything.

Blackstone took a pinch of snuff from a gold Nathaniel Mills box given to him by a woman. 'That's surely not the only reason I'm quartered in Kensington Palace like a servant.'

'No,' Birnie admitted. 'Not quite. Have you noticed anything suspicious?'

'Not a damn thing.'

'Has the Duke of Cumberland been around to see the family?'

'Not that I know of.'

'Hmmm.' Birnie took a light from the jumping flames of the fire and relit his pipe. 'The Duchess's real fear is that Cumberland will try and kidnap or kill the Princess.' He pointed the smoke-dribbling stem of his pipe. 'And I must warn you, Blackstone, that this is in the strictest confidence. No one must be told of her fears.'

Blackstone, remembering the keen hearing of the plump-breasted girl in the Brown Bear, assured him that no one would be told. Implying that no one would want to know about the Duchess's theories.

'It's not just the Duchess,' Birnie said.

Blackstone looked up. 'Who else?'

'Sir John Conroy, the Master of the Household. You've met him, I presume?'

'Yes, I've met him. But he didn't tell me anything about any suspicions.'

'He will. He wanted to have a look at you first.'

'So I was on approval?'

'You were.'

'I hope he liked what he saw?'

'He did and he's asked me to supply you with the details. That's why I summoned you here. Did you place a guard on the Princess before you left?'

Blackstone nodded. 'One member of the Foot Patrol outside the room where little Drina is in bed with a cold. But without his redbreast and the rest of his uniform.'

'That wouldn't please Peel,' Birnie said happily.

'It didn't please him.'

'I'm afraid the evidence isn't very strong.'

'I understand, sir.' Their enjoyment of the patrolman's anger had established a bond.

'Sir John Conroy also suspects the Duke of Cumberland.'

'Uncle Ernest. Why?'

'You know something about the Duke, I presume?'

'I know he's supposed to have butchered his valet. I know he's supposed to be sadistic, incestuous, perverted and horribly scarred and blind in one eye. You could say he has handicaps.'

Birnie said: 'He's also un-British.'

Blackstone looked to see if he was joking, but he couldn't be sure. 'Do we have any evidence at all of a plot?'

'The Princess has been a little poorly of late, hasn't she?'

Blackstone said she had. Growing pains, he thought.

'Not poison?'

'I shouldn't think so. It hadn't occurred to me.'

'It has occurred to the Duchess and Sir John.'

'With any medical support?'

'Not yet. But her bread and milk is being analysed.' Birnie sounded embarrassed.

'Good God! And her sweets?'

'That will be enough. It might sound ridiculous but we're talking about the future Queen.'

Blackstone stood up and walked to the window. Across the road the Brown Bear bulged with boozy custom; laughter and the sound of broken glass reaching him faintly. A lamplighter passed; central London assembled in deathly gaslight; crime stirred. And here am I discussing poisoned bread and milk. He took another pinch of snuff, hand feeling the smooth engine-turned warmth of the box and vaguely remembering the woman's body.

Birnie said: 'Cumberland is a ruthless man, as you've pointed out. Has it occurred to you that the only person standing between him and eventual accession to the throne is the Princess?'

'Hardly evidence of intent, sir.'

'We have to act on suspicion, Blackstone.'

'Is there nothing else to add substance to it?'

'The Duchess has noticed suspicious characters around the Palace.'

'Such as who?'

'No one in particular. On her walks . . . you know . . .'

'Yes,' Blackstone said, remembering the pretty, distraught face. Pretty, distraught *German* face! According to Page, Germans had a habit of scratching their heads with dinner forks.

'Obviously we have to give them the protection they ask for. After all, we should be well satisfied these days that the Duchess asked for us by name.'

'I suppose so.'

Blackstone, sensing fractional loss of authority in Birnie, walked around the office looking at the pictures. Thomas de Veil, the first police chief magistrate served by corrupt parish constables, informers and thief-takers; married four times, father of twenty-five children, fond of taking women suspects into the closet for questioning. Henry Fielding, magistrate and author of *Tom Jones*, who started the Runners with the legend 'Quick notice and sudden pursuit' and proposed the first criminal register. His blind half-brother John who founded the 'Quarterly Pursuit' now called 'The Public Hue and Cry' with its lists of stolen property, wanted criminals and Army deserters. Sampson Wright and the others who had won money and authority for the Runners. And respect.

'Yes, I suppose so,' Blackstone said again.

Birnie said: 'Sit down, Blackstone,' retrieving his authority. 'So I want you to return to Kensington Palace and keep an eye open. Report anything suspicious. And let me know if Cumberland makes an appearance.'

'He shouldn't be difficult to recognize,' Blackstone observed.

'One other thing. The whole Palace is aware of your presence. So we'll have to establish someone inside.'

'An *agent provocateur*?'

'If you like.' Birnie didn't care for foreign phrases.

'Another Runner?'

Birnie shook his head. 'We can't afford another. No' – his voice was reluctant – 'it will have to be one of your friends, Blackstone.'

'You mean one of my contacts from my past, sir.' The past that never sank.

'Someone who can get himself into service in the Palace.'

'None of my *friends* could manage that, sir. They don't have the right qualifications. Not for honest, decent work. What would they do for references?'

'Forge them,' Birnie said. 'Handley should be able to help you when he comes back from his murder in Fetcham. He is, after all, our fraud specialist. But the references will have to commend the highest qualities in your man. Can you find a man who has the appearance to go with such a reference?' He looked doubtful. 'Here, see what I mean.' He tossed the *Morning Post* across the desk.

Blackstone read the advertisement that Birnie had marked. 'Wanted Immediately Cook and Housekeeper that the utmost excellence in either capacity would not answer, without corresponding perfection in both; accompanied by absolute sobriety and universal honesty. Her age must be from 25–40. In regard to her character, that of the last service, unless it has been a long one, will not suffice. The Advertiser being of the opinion that all the malefactions of Mankind originate in practical falsehood, gives warning that the first lie shall be the last . . .'

Birnie smiled: sunlight on the moors. 'I imagine it would give Handley great pleasure to falsify a reference for that job.'

'It looks like a vacancy in heaven,' Blackstone said. He brushed specks of soot from his tight, tailored trousers. 'None of my friends could match up to anything like that. Nor could a nun, for that matter.'

'In the first place,' Birnie said, 'it's a man we want. In the second place you will receive some assistance from inside the Palace in getting your friend a job.'

'I thought you said it was secret, sir.'

'To you, me and one other – Sir John Conroy. He will advise the house steward to take your man. Have you thought of anyone?'

A gallery of villainy presented itself before Blackstone. One more villainous than the others, although only to the knowledgeable, such as himself.

'There is one, sir.'

Birnie held up his hand. 'I don't want to know his name, Blackstone. There are too many people snooping into our affairs, our methods. There's talk of yet another House of Commons Committee. Instigated by Peel, no doubt. He'll blacken us in every way possible. Then merge the horse and foot patrols and the Thames Police into one. Then us, Blackstone. He'll be after us because he won't be able to do without us.' He checked himself. 'But will your man look vaguely like an honest, respectable servant?'

'Vaguely,' Blackstone said.

Birnie picked up his pen to terminate the interview. 'I think that's about it, Blackstone.' He held the quill like an arrow in his schoolmaster's fingers. 'But don't forget – if anything happens to the Princess it will be the end of the Bow Street Runners.'

Not the end of the heir to the throne, Blackstone noted.

He rose and left the tough old bastard scratching away with his pen, his body severed by a stratum of soot-laden coal smoke, surrounded by pictures of the tough old bastards who had preceded him.

Chapter Three

IT was difficult to tell about Lawler. No one was quite sure about him, except, perhaps, Blackstone. People were left with an impression of sharpness, an uneasy suspicion that they had given themselves away – a phrase, a gesture, a hesitancy. Lawler inserted himself painlessly like a needle-sharp stiletto that is hardly felt until death. When Lawler left a room people checked their pockets, even if he hadn't been near them.

Nor could they always describe him exactly afterwards. If shopkeepers were around they presumed he was one; if lawyers were around they seemed to remember him in a wig. In fact, he was presentable, thirtyish and dark. But only striking because of the unease he left behind.

He earned his living through gambling, taking wagers more than laying them. He accepted wagers on anything from cock-fighting to cricket. It was through cricket that he first met Blackstone. The M.C.C. v. Norfolk at Lord's when William Ward scored over 200. There had been a wager and Lawler had lost. Later at Lawler's home Blackstone had asked to be paid, his fingers round Lawler's windpipe.

At the same time Blackstone had discovered something about Lawler. Something which could have resulted in the House of Correction followed by transportation. Neither could wholly remember what it was. But the relationship had remained; and the payments for information and help.

If Lawler respected anyone it was Blackstone. If he ever needed a friend – which he never had – then it would, he hoped, be Blackstone.

25

Except that Blackstone never showed any sign of warmth.

Lawler lived in a one-room basement in the Rookery at Holborn, furnished with stolen property. The walls were covered with sporting prints covering the crawling cracks, and trophies – the wicket-keeping gloves allegedly worn by J. Bernard (Eton and West Kent), a blood-stained prizefighter's overcoat ... In one corner stood a thrush imprisoned in a cage; in another a pan of sausages, a lamp, and a tinderbox.

Lawler greeted Blackstone without surprise and pointed at the gin, hot water and sugar. 'Fancy a nip, Mr Blackstone?'

'No thanks, Lawler.'

'What can I do for you, Mr Blackstone?'

'I need some help.'

Lawler nodded, filling his mouth with sausage. Blackstone waited, looking at the gin which he would have drunk if there had been a clean cup.

Lawler, who liked a chat, said: 'I see they're going to experiment with that round-arm bowling next year. Can't see it catching on myself.'

'It will.' Blackstone enjoyed cricket and gambled moderately at Lord's where he had recently kept a clergyman accused of welshing on his bets under surveillance. 'But it will slow up the scoring.'

Lawler finished his sausages and poured himself gin. 'It's just not cricket,' he complained. 'Are you going to any fights? And if you are, have you got any tips?'

Five years earlier Blackstone had tipped him that Tom Hickman, the Gas-light Man, would beat the knock-kneed Bill Neate. Neate had slaughtered Hickman over eighteen rounds – Hickman's face had been compared to a death's-head spouting blood – and Lawler had spent weeks dodging his creditors.

Blackstone said: 'Luckily for you I haven't.'

'Not lucky, Mr Blackstone. As soon as you give me a tip I lay money on the other fellow.'

'I haven't come to see you about betting this time, Lawler.'

Lawler expressed surprise because it was around the cock-fighting pits, skittle alleys and prizefighting rings that Blackstone generally asked him to operate. 'What is it then, Mr Blackstone. Do you want me to rob a bank, on my life?'

'No, Lawler, I want you to go into service.' He smiled despite everything.

Three gins later, after much incredulity, Blackstone succeeded in making Lawler believe him.

Lawler said: 'I can't, Mr Blackstone. I just can't.'

'You don't want to spend tonight in the cells, do you?'

'On what charge?'

'Charge? There doesn't have to be a charge, Lawler, and you know it. A suspected person or a reputed thief found wandering in the streets. If the magistrate decided that you "had intent to commit a felony" then he could give you six months under the Vagrancy Act. Not,' he added with candour, 'that we Runners have any constitutional status.'

'So how can you threaten me?'

'Anyone can arrest anyone, Lawler. You know that. Or I could enlist the support of the parish constable.'

Lawler said he didn't think that would be necessary.

Blackstone added: 'And, of course, the payment would be quite liberal.'

'What had you in mind?'

'Five sovereigns,' Blackstone said.

Lawler shook his nothing face decisively. 'Five yellow boys? For that price impossible, Mr Blackstone. What do you get for looking after the Princess, Mr Blackstone. Not much less than £200 a year, I'll wager.'

Blackstone remembered that £200 was the price in 1786. And he wasn't getting much more now. 'Even if it was, that's only about £4 a week.'

'But that's not all you get, Mr Blackstone. Far from it, if I'm not mistaken. Some of the Runners die very rich men, I believe.'

'You believe too much,' Blackstone said. 'I'll give you £10. The alternative is six months for wandering abroad.'

'But I'm not wandering.'

'Would you care to bet on that?'

Lawler shrugged. 'I'll do my best. You can't say better than that. But I can't promise anything. What am I to be?'

'A footman. An under-footman. Second or third probably. You'll get a uniform, victuals including beer and about £20 a year.'

'A year? I'm not going into service for a year. You wouldn't wish that on me, Mr Blackstone, would you?'

Faintly, Blackstone could already hear the dual personality of a footman emerging: arrogance to anyone infinitesimally inferior in station, servility to all superiors. The chameleon Lawler was already adapting.

Blackstone cajoled. 'Think of the way you'll be getting your information. Just like the footmen Jonathan Wild used to employ. Making love to the dolly-mops, Lawler. Think about that.'

Lawler thought about it and was moved. Lawler the developing manservant that is; the real Lawler – if such a person existed – liked women, but he preferred fast horses.

'What sort of work would I have to do?' the superior footman asked.

'God knows. Deliver messages, wait outside theatres, carry in the roast to the dinner table, cut the ice from the river for the ice-house.'

'Not carrying chamber-pots, I hope.'

'That's housemaids' work. Along with sweeping the carpets with wet tea-leaves and polishing the door-knockers. No, Lawler, no chamber-pots.'

'And my uniform?'

'The fashion of gentlemen of the last century. Knee breeches, silk stockings with buckles, embroidered coat with shoulder knots, powdered wig . . .' Blackstone sickened of it. 'In fact, Lawler, you'll look beautiful.'

Lawler made himself some more hot gin. In the corner the thrush sang sweetly and hopelessly. 'I'd do it if I thought I was up to it. On my life I would.'

'You'll do it anyway,' Blackstone said. 'I'll be the man above stairs, you'll be the one below. I'll interview the other servants but you mustn't take any notice of that. I'll be burrowing down, you'll be burrowing up. When we meet at the top of the area steps we should have the answer. One way or the other.'

Down the road Blackstone stopped at a stall selling kidney pies and baked potatoes. Every time the pieman opened the oven, sparks dashed out and lost themselves in the night.

The pieman had long greasy hair and wore a crusty apron over his waistcoat and breeches. He had one good eye and a socket that fascinated children.

'You should wear a patch over that thing,' Blackstone said, biting into the potato and feeling the steam fill his mouth.

'The children wouldn't like that, Blackie.'

'You might get more customers.'

'I get enough. Business is better now the nights are drawing in.' He scrubbed some potatoes and pushed them into the oven; sparks escaped like trapped insects. Then he said: 'Do you mind a word of advice, Blackie?'

'Not from you. Not from anyone who makes pies as good as these.' He removed flakes of crust from his lips.

'Get out of this area, Blackie. You're too flash in your fine clothes. A lot of people round these parts have got it in for you. You know that.'

'And I've got it in for them.'

'But there's only one of you.'

'But I carry this.' Blackstone picked up his baton bearing the gilt crown.

'So you do. So you do. But I ask you – what good is a baton against a life-preserver, a barker, a stiletto?'

'And I've got this.' Blackstone slapped one of the pistols in his pockets. 'It's good of you, Harry, but I can take care of myself.'

The pieman shook his head. 'Such brave words, my dear.' He served an old woman who looked suspiciously at Blackstone from beneath her shawl before hobbling away, carrying a potato in leathery hands that hardly felt the heat, or anything else. He went on: '*I can take care of myself.* They sound like famous last words, Blackie.'

'I took care of myself and you once, Harry. Remember?'

'I remember. I wouldn't have this other good glim if it wasn't for you. And probably no head neither. But you were in the Foot Patrol in those days, Blackie, before they gave 'em those fancy waistcoats. You were just doing a job. They remembered you was one of them and they was proud of you.' Harry Tyler considered his words. 'Well, almost proud. As proud as anyone in the Rookery can be of one of their own who takes to the law. But that was before you turned on them, Blackie. Now they reckon you've betrayed them.'

'Maybe I have. I'm a traitor to every bastard who sticks four-year-old kids up chimneys, a traitor to every bastard who gives thirteen-year-old girls to rich gentlemen for their pleasure, a traitor to every bastard who works children from five in the morning till ten at night . . .'

'Fond of young 'uns aren't you, Blackie?'

'I was one myself once,' Blackstone said.

He picked up his baton, felt his pistols. 'And I'll be a traitor to every landlord grabbing the last penny from the starving before chucking them out on the street, a traitor to every crooked parish constable . . .'

'Another word of advice,' Tyler said, 'from one who owes his life to you.'

'What's that, Harry?'

'Don't get too noble, Blackie.'

Shadows moved beyond the penumbra of gaslight. At the base of the lamps children slept, or played marbles or begged – an unrewarding pastime in this part of London.

The cobblestones felt hard under his buckled shoes and he fancied he could smell the Thames above the smell of the slums. A few prostitutes approached him, but fell away when they saw his clothes: he was not the sort of customer you lifted your skirts for in the Rookery.

He kept to the centre of the road, as far as possible from the shadows, hand close to the butt of a pistol. Past brightly-lit chandlers selling coffee and tea, past a woman with a baby singing ballads. In the distance he heard a boy selling muffins.

Gradually he formed the impression that one particular shadow was accompanying him. He stopped: all movement stopped as abruptly as a cat stops twittering birds. He walked on, hand on the pistol: movement and noise returned.

Imagination? The words of Harry Tyler lingered. . . . Blackstone remembered his last arrest in St Giles. A boarding-house keeper who had packed fifty girls and boys into one room at 1d a night; one morning he had cleared them out but one had remained. Dead. Suffocated. But difficult to indict the landlord. So Blackstone had arraigned him for theft, assisted by two false witnesses, and he was now in a gaol where conditions were a little better than they were in his boarding-house.

There had been others. Some free and looking for revenge. Not to mention the friends and relatives of the imprisoned. . . .

Ahead, the leaning houses looked a little better kept. The road a little wider. The lamps flaring brighter, or so it seemed. Now he fancied that the pursuing shadow had a shuffle all of its own. He turned into a tavern, ordered some ale and waited.

The other customers continued talking, but he knew most of them had changed the topics when he entered. No one could be that interested in the weather. One or two who were drunk jeered, but not too boldly; when he glanced at them they turned away. Blackstone enjoyed it. Why not? The words of Harry Tyler returned. 'Don't get too noble.' Surely I'm not that much of a hypocrite. But you could never be too sure with yourself. He left his tankard half full of ale and returned to the night.

Across the road the shuffling. Like a body being pulled over the cobbles, or a sack of dismembered limbs. But there was nothing there, only a stray dog sleeping on a grill emitting warm fumes. He threw a handful of coins to some children playing with horse-chestnuts and walked on. The shuffle remained as persistent as a conscience.

He considered returning to his room at Kensington Palace. Then thought: to hell with it. The Foot Patrolman could remain there for the night. He would return to his own rooms in Paddington village.

A hackney-carriage clattered past. Blackstone hailed it with his baton. The driver peered down. 'Blackstone, isn't it?'

'It is.'

'Where do you want to go?'

Blackstone told him.

'Are you in a paying mood tonight, Mr Blackstone?'

'I'll think about it,' Blackstone said, climbing in.

He hoped he had left the shadow behind.

It may have been the same shadow who had followed in another hackney; or it may have been a different shadow. Whichever it was, it gained substance outside his home.

Blackstone flung himself sideways as the club swung, missing him and striking the railings above the area.

The assailant, cloaked and masked by a handkerchief, swung again. This time the club caught Blackstone on the shoulder, numbing his arm, the bone saved by the thick material of his coat. He fell against the railings, reaching for his pistol. But the man kicked it away, swinging again with the club made from the butt of a carbine.

The hackney driver's whip lashed out encircling his throat like an octopus's tentacle. The man choked and fought the tentacle. Blackstone kicked him in the crotch and dived for his pistol. But the man was free of the whip and he came at Blackstone, who was trying to pick up his pistol with his good left hand. He stamped, catching Blackstone's thumb with his heel, almost cracking the bone.

But Blackstone had his ankle. He jerked and the man fell, a knife flashing in his hand like a silver fish. The knife slashed and opened up Blackstone's new coat.

Again the whip whistled out; but this time it tied itself round a railing. Blackstone brought his knee up, finding the crotch

32

again. The man's belly convulsed as if he were going to vomit. Blackstone reached for the gun, but the man was on his feet.

Blackstone pointed the pistol from the ground. 'Don't move or I'll blow your head off.'

The man jumped to one side and ran. Blackstone fired but he wasn't left-handed. A flash of daylight, a crack of thunder. The ball whistled through the branches of a tree towards the stars as the man ran zig-zag down the street until he was a shadow once more.

Blackstone chased but gave up because it was useless.

When he returned, one arm hanging like a pendulum, the driver was still there. 'Are you all right, Mr Blackstone?'

'I'm all right. Thanks for your help.'

'Lucky for you,' the driver said, 'that you paid your fare this time.'

He stripped to the waist and examined his shoulder. Nothing to be done but await the onset of feeling, and pain. His coat was damaged more than his body.

He brewed tea and patrolled the sitting-room wondering what it was about his assailant. A sense of familiarity. But what? The man had only choked and he had been masked. Smell, touch . . .

Restlessly he moved around touching the possessions that he collected rather than bought. Soft leather books with vellum pages which he never read: a stuffed green-scalped mallard in a glass case; an oval looking-glass set in a complicated gold frame; a folding screen writhing with Chinese dragons; chairs and settee upholstered in red and white stripes; mahogany chest of drawers. And his collection of guns on the walls and in the drawers.

I know him. The familiarity lingered like woodsmoke on clothes. But the more he concentrated the more elusive the identity became.

He took some snuff and was relieved when he heard a knock on the door.

The girl from the Brown Bear said: 'My, aren't we grand.'

But the cheek had left her voice. She said: 'Aren't you going to put a shirt on?'

He shook his head. And began to help her to get on equal terms.

Chapter Four

———————— ◆ ————————

CONSCIENTIOUSLY, but without enthusiasm, Blackstone set about questioning the servants. He told them that the miniature the King had given to the Princess was missing, and arranged to have it locked up.

One of the main hindrances was the Princess's mother, the former Serene Highness Victoria Mary Louisa, daughter of the Duke of Saxe-Coburg Saalfeld, widow of both Emich Charles, Prince of Leiningen, and his Royal Highness the Duke of Kent, who had died eight months after the birth of his daughter.

Blackstone found her to be a pest.

She suspected all the English servants and told the German staff to watch them. She interrupted his questioning, then questioned him about his deductions in English as painful as chalk screeching on a blackboard. She was such an inexorable pest that he was surprised to find he had developed some compassion for her. For her muddle of lap-dogs and song-birds, her excessive anxieties, her imaginary persecutions.

Even more surprisingly friendship developed between them; although he felt sure that at first she had suspected him, too.

Once, as they stood at a window in the south-east wing of the Palace, alive with the ticking of clocks, she confided in him. In thick accents. Tortuously and emotionally.

The Duke of Kent had only married her in the hope that she might conceive England's next monarch. But love had developed between them – then he had died. She had stood alone with her baby, and her other daughter, Princess Feodore, in a hostile land. Even at the christening at the gold font in the Cupola Room of the Palace George IV, then Prince Regent, had refused to give the baby the Christian names she wanted. After an embarrassing silence he had muttered, 'Alexandrina'. Finally he had also consented to Victoria, after her mother, on the condition that it came after Alexandrina in deference to the Tsar of Russia.

Tears trickled down her cheeks. Outside, on the frost-sugared lawn beside Kensington Gardens, Drina rode a pony watched by Fräulein Lehzen, chewing caraway seeds as usual, Princess Feodore, the late Duke of Kent's sister Princess Augusta Sophia, the head nurse and, in the background, the new under-footman, Lawler.

'If only people had been more friendly,' the Duchess said. 'I thank God for Sir John Conroy.'

'I'm sure they meant to be, ma'am,' Blackstone assured her. 'It's just the difficulties of language.'

'I've tried to be a good mother. Did you know that we almost lost Drina before my husband was taken from me?'

Hastily Blackstone said he did know that, vaguely remembering a report of an accident in Sidmouth, Devon, when a boy had fired some pellets through the Princess's window.

'I've done everything for England that my husband would have wished.' And she recounted how the Duke of Kent had personally driven their shabby old coach all the way from the Castle of Amorbach to Kensington to ensure that his daughter was born on English soil.

Blackstone scanned the Gardens for any sign of interested strangers. No one. He was thirsty and bored. He felt sorry for the worrying woman beside him, but sympathy didn't necessarily embrace interest. He fought a yawn and listened on. How Drina had been the first member of the Royal family to be vaccinated against smallpox, how she had been 'fed the natural way', how she loved cradle songs, how well she now spoke English, how well she read the Bible with her preceptor, the Rev. George Davys, how imperiously she held her head as a result of a piece of holly being tied just below her throat. . . .

The clocks ticked on. A dog barked, a lost mongrel bark on

the autumn air. Wednesday. Soon Prince Leopold would be here from Esher. Drina's favourite uncle, as cracked as any of the Royal eccentrics with his boa feathers and three-inch soles to his shoes. He hoped that the Duchess wouldn't ask him to question Uncle Leopold.

Together they paced the yellow carpet of the homely old red-brick Palace reconstructed by Christopher Wren. Conspirators in what should have been a cheerful middle-class German family if the little girl ordering the page around on the lawn hadn't been heir to the throne after the Duke of Clarence.

'What can be done, Mr Blackstone? What can we do?'

'We must change the Princess's timetable.'

'A good idea, Mr Blackstone. At the moment we breakfast at 8.30. After that the Princess Alexandrina Victoria goes for an hour's drive or walk. Then I instruct her from ten to twelve. I insist on simplicity of diet. . . .'

Blackstone managed a respectful interruption. 'Then you should breakfast at different times and rearrange her timetable by say fifteen minutes every day.'

He thought: And now I sound as if I'm taking it seriously.

He said: 'May I ask you, ma'am, a little more about the basis of your suspicions?'

'Have you met the Duke of Cumberland, Mr Blackstone?'

'No, ma'am. But I've heard of him and I wouldn't want him for a godfather.'

'He's an evil man, Mr Blackstone. And he means to prevent my daughter from acceding to the throne after the death of King William.'

'But the Duke of Clarence isn't King William yet.'

'But he will be and when he is Alexandrina Victoria will almost certainly become Queen after him. If anything happens to her then Cumberland will be King. Can you imagine that, Mr Blackstone? A murderer on the throne of England.'

'No, ma'am, I can't.' He paused. 'But is there nothing else that has aroused your suspicions?'

'The Princess has been ill lately.'

'I've interviewed her doctor and he diagnosed a feverish cold.'

'It could just as easily have been the symptoms of poison. So you must persevere, Mr Blackstone. For the sake of England,' she added in her German voice.

Blackstone said he would do all he could and tried to break away; but she stopped him, pointing out of the window. 'Who is that footman? I don't know him. Who is he, Mr Blackstone?'

'I believe his name is Lawler, Your Highness.'

'Then question him, Mr Blackstone, and let me know what you think about him. I don't like the look of him.'

Which showed a certain acumen, Blackstone thought.

The house steward, butler and other senior servants – employed since Parliament had granted the Duchess an extra £6,000 – were indignant when he told them he was investigating the theft of the miniature. But they calmed down when he aimed the gilt-crowned baton at them.

The butler tried to be tougher. But old inherited knowledge stirred within Blackstone. 'Are you happy in your work here?' he asked.

'I am and I don't see what it's got to do with you.'

'I told Sir John Conroy what a nice drop of claret we had the other night.'

'I'm honoured,' the butler said sarcastically.

'I didn't say that it seemed to have been reclaimed by someone popping a dozen pippins in it.'

'How did you know that?'

Blackstone shrugged.

'And in any case there's nothing wrong with that,' the butler said.

'I didn't say there was. Nor did I tell the head steward that I thought that too much laundry-blue had been applied to the plums . . .'

'How the hell do you know about these things.'

Blackstone waved his baton like a wand. 'Let's get on with the questions.'

The housekeeper was also on her dignity. But he took a glass of British Champagne, brewed from unripe gooseberries and brandy, with her in her room and she relented, advising Blackstone to concentrate on a lady's-maid called Irma.

He also interviewed Lawler to maintain the pretence.

And when the servants were all working he let himself into their rooms, into the cells containing the parishes of their aspirations.

In a housemaid's room candles, scissors, thimble, a 3d novel and a 6d play, a Bible, a photograph of a country boy beneath the pillow, a tortoiseshell comb, a print of the Crucifixion above the bed.

He also picked the lock of THE BOX. Inside – clothes, books about dreams, some country money, a picture of a soldier locked away as if the country boy might spot him, letters tied with ribbon, a song-book, some gingerbread nuts and a poem that the soldier or the country-boy had written to her.

Shamefacedly Blackstone closed THE BOX.

In other rooms he found evidence of petty theft and, in the butler's, pornographic inclination. Nothing significant. Not one flitting moth of suspicion. He grew more sick of it and decided to see Birnie again. But first the inquiries had to be complete. And that meant interviewing some of the aristocracy at the Palace. To his disgust Blackstone found that he had been delaying this on purpose. Subconsciously but purposely. You seem to know your place, Blackie.

But first Blackstone told the Duchess that he would have to talk to Princess Alexandrina Victoria. Reluctantly the Duchess agreed on the understanding that Blackstone didn't convey the reason for the questions. And didn't address her as the future Queen of England, a fate of which she was presumed to have no inkling.

You were, Blackstone thought, either anti-social or sycophantic. You had to choose your attitude in your dealings with the aristocracy. But as most of the aristocrats visited the Palace for sycophantic purposes Blackstone chose the anti-social course –

backed by the power of his magic wand. In any case aristocrats had their ways of avoiding public scandal after arrest. The rustle of notes, the carriage waiting outside. But not, he believed, with Birnie.

Of all the titled personages present the only one he could stomach was Sir John Conroy. He had been the Duke of Kent's equerry and he'd got the post as head of the household because the Duke wished it. Blackstone warmed to the Anglo-Irishman because he sensed that they shared a similar apprenticeship to success, the same fear of return. Also Conroy had simple tastes: drinking and women.

After himself, Sir John Conroy, a virile-looking man with a cleft chin, placed the Princess next on his priorities. Blackstone liked this, too. He also admired the ex-Army captain's lack of servility in dealing with the Germans, from the Duchess downwards.

Sir John was present when Blackstone talked to Princess Alexandrina Victoria. As was the Duchess of Kent, worry folding her pretty face.

They sat in the nursery with its dark wallpaper – repetitive pictures of a blacksmith shoeing a placid horse – and its wooden dolls.

The Princess had clusters of fair curls, brilliant blue eyes and an arrogant manner. A precocious brat; but a Queen, he supposed.

The questions didn't come easily.

'Your Royal Highness, have you noticed anything suspicious at all?'

'Suspicious? What do you mean suspicious? What does he mean, mama?' A trace of a departing German accent still there.

'Any strangers around when you're on your walks.'

'Of course not. I wouldn't notice them anyway,' the future Queen added. She smiled suddenly at Blackstone. 'What are you doing here, Mr Blackstone? You're so different from the others.'

Blackstone smiled. You could accept that any way you wanted.

The Princess said: 'You're not as serious as everyone else.'
She lowered her voice. 'Fräulein Lehzen is very serious and
eats caraway seeds all the time.'

'Drina,' the Duchess said sharply, 'please behave yourself.
I'm afraid she's showing off,' she told Blackstone.

'Little girls often do,' Blackstone said.

'I'm not a little girl.'

Sir John Conroy said: 'You are a little girl and if you
don't behave yourself you won't have Lablache to teach you
singing.'

'Good,' said Her Royal Highness. She turned to Blackstone.
'Will you come up and play with me sometimes?'

'I should love to,' Blackstone lied.

'Good. Then that shall be arranged.'

Blackstone terminated the questioning and they let in
Fräulein Lehzen, the flowers and frills on her cap shivering
with agitation, her Adam's apple a second chin.

In his chambers Sir John Conroy offered champagne. Blackstone declined it. 'I'd like some rum and hot water if you
have it.'

Conroy grinned. 'A good idea. Champagne becomes a habit.
But it's not a man's drink.'

'I'll drink to the day when there's any possibility of champagne becoming a habit.'

'You're not doing badly, Blackstone. Stop feeling sorry for
yourself.'

Was he? Yes, he supposed he was.

Conroy sipped his rum. 'We're paying you enough anyway.
And judging by all the mention you get in the newspapers you
must be worth a few guineas.' He leaned forward in his chair.
'I like your tailor. Where do you go?'

Blackstone gave him an address in St James's.

Conroy made a note of it and suggested that one evening
they should go up West together. The Strangers' Club and then
perhaps Astley's. Find some girls. 'You a Runner, me a knight
and almost a baronet – we can't go wrong.'

They drank to it, their alliance warm and spicy over the hot rum.

After a while Blackstone asked him about his suspicions.

Conroy became serious. 'It's Cumberland. I believe Birnie told you.'

'He didn't tell me anything specific.'

'There isn't anything specific. But you know what these circles are like. A friend of Cumberland's came visiting here and told me Uncle Ernest was planning to kidnap the Princess.'

'And you took the threat seriously?'

Conroy shrugged. 'Not necessarily. But you don't take risks when the future Queen of England is involved.'

'Nothing else?'

'She hasn't been too well lately. . . .'

Blackstone said: 'I hope, Sir John, you're not going to tell me about her bread and milk being poisoned.'

A clause or two of their alliance was scrapped.

'Look, Blackstone, don't try and ridicule this. There may be nothing in it, I don't know. But I mean to make it my business to ensure that the Princess reaches the throne. It's about time this country had a decent monarch. And she'll be one, mark my words. She's a fine little girl. And her father was a fine man. If you think this job is beneath your dignity please tell me.'

Blackstone sipped his rum, Nelson's Blood. 'It's beneath my dignity,' he said.

'Then I'll ask Birnie to find me another Runner.'

'Please do.' Blackstone stood up. 'I'm not a nursemaid.' He picked up his baton and walked towards the door.

Conroy stopped him. 'On second thoughts I won't ask him. What do you want – more money?'

Blackstone thought that perhaps he did. 'Why have you changed your mind?'

'Because Birnie reckons you're the best he's got.'

Pleasure spurted as warmly as the rum. 'Thank you, Sir John.'

He closed the door and walked down the corridor listening to the clocks ticking their suspicions.

On the whole the aristocracy accepted the questioning rather better than the senior menials. Understanding the difficulty of Blackstone's job and often allowing him as much as ten minutes of their time; sometimes he obtained a longer audience with a gesture of his hand.

The society into which he peered had its capitals at St James's, Windsor, Brighton, Kensington . . . its outposts in ancestral homes. Its members knew nothing of Bethnal Green, Poplar or the Dials and only a little of Cubitt's new buildings going up in Belgravia. The unrest among the workers wasn't their concern. Some hadn't even heard of Francis Place's work two years earlier on the Combination Act's repeal which allowed workers to form trade unions. Nor had they paused to consider the dark hours children worked in factories and mines. London mobs clamouring for Catholic emancipation or higher wages were aggravations which their coachmen had to avoid.

They were a little more aware of foreign matters: President Monroe's new 'doctrine', the treaty between Britain and Russia, the Greek-Turkish troubles in which Lord Byron had died. And some domestic matters such as the new steam railway between Stockton and Darlington.

But the real fabric of their society was Royal gossip, which was provided generously by George IV. They gossiped about his mistresses, Mrs Fitzherbert in particular, about his drunkenness, about his dirty talk, which the Grand Duchess Catherine of Russia had commented upon.

They gossiped about the Succession after the King's death and the death of his brother, William, which couldn't be all that far ahead.

And so they settled on Kensington Palace.

Blackstone, observing the courtiers, felt profoundly sorry for Princess Alexandrina Victoria, 37th in descent from Egbert, the first sole monarch of England, if she reached the throne.

After the third or fourth chat with the peers, knights and honourables, Blackstone's pity began to intrude.

He took it out first on Sir Rupert Charlston, confidant of Sir William Knighton, the doctor, Keeper of the Privy Purse and confidant of the King.

Charlston, who was always around the Palace, was a tall, powerful man, with long sandy hair; a deep-voiced raconteur, swordsman, bon viveur and a chancer.

He was also a middle-ageing womanizer who hadn't yet divulged his age to himself. He was so big that he looked ungainly, a tree that could be knocked flat by the wind.

'And now,' he said, stretching, 'I have to go. I have an appointment.'

'With your bookmaker?' Blackstone was glad that he had taken the precaution of investigating Charlston's habits – and discovered the gambling debts.

'Yes, as it happens. Not that it's any business of yours.'

Blackstone took some snuff from the gold box monogrammed with his initials. 'It could be my business.'

Charlston sat back in the chair which looked too fragile for his weight. 'Really? In what way?'

'You owe a lot of money, don't you, Sir Rupert?'

The weight shifted and the chair creaked. 'Surely you can do better than that, Blackstone.'

Blackstone said he could. He opened the drawer of the desk in the study which had been set aside for him and took out a sheet of paper. 'You lost £500 on the Derby. You lost another £500 on the first Eton–Winchester cricket match. You . . .'

'I know how much I lost, Blackstone. Morgan shouldn't have told you.'

'The bookmaker? He didn't,' Blackstone said, acknowledging the worth of Lawler's contacts. 'About £3,000, isn't it?'

Charlston shrugged. 'Perhaps. It might be more, it might be less. Nothing that I can't win back with interest tomorrow.'

'Provided you have the money to wager.'

'You needn't concern yourself with that.' Charlston yawned. 'Now the devil take you and your prying ways – I'm leaving.' He stood up.

Blackstone took out a Barton pocket pistol and placed it

carefully on the desk beside his baton. 'Not just yet, Sir Rupert.'

'You think you can stop me?'

Blackstone tapped the flintlock. 'This can. So please don't be dramatic.' He paused. 'You know, I can always spot a fraud, Sir Rupert.'

Charlston imposed himself on the chair again. 'And I can always spot a slander.'

'I'm not questioning your title. Just your values.'

'I think,' Charlston said, 'that we should settle this the traditional way. Would seven o'clock tomorrow morning suit you?' He smiled. 'Then we'll *both* be armed.'

'Delighted,' Blackstone said. 'But not tomorrow. Not while I'm on duty here.' He spoke with regret because the prospect of humiliating (not necessarily killing) Charlston was pleasing. 'You know as well as I do that duelling is against the law and that it's the duty of the Runners to prevent it.'

'Is it really?' Charlston said.

'But when this is over I'll break the law just so that I can break you.'

'I'll be waiting, Blackstone. But don't make it too long. Now, what do you want of me?'

Blackstone leaned across the desk. 'A little prying on my behalf, Sir Rupert. I think you'll be quite a good pupil. As you know, I don't like you and I don't like your sort. You're only here making up to this quaint German mob because you want to be on the winning side. But you don't give a damn about the Princess.' He paused. 'But I do.'

'Very touching,' Charlston said.

'I don't think a £3,000 gambling debt would be very much appreciated in Court circles.'

'Blackmail, Blackstone?'

'It goes with my name.'

Charlston crossed his legs, thighs muscular above his knee breeches. 'No one would believe you.'

'Don't flatter yourself. In any case I could prove it quite easily.'

'Supposing I have a lucky bet tomorrow?'

'As I said, I don't fancy you have the money to wager, Sir Rupert. And if you have – where has the money come from? From the sale of a miniature belonging to the Princess?'

'Do you think I stole it?'

Hardly, Blackstone thought, because it wasn't missing. He said: 'It's not what I think. It's what your Royal contacts might think. I think, Sir Rupert, that you would very shortly find yourself out in the cold.'

Charlston considered this. Then he asked: 'What do you want me to pry into?'

'I believe you manage to mix with Cumberland as well as Kennington.'

'I know Uncle Ernest,' Charlston said. 'And I know most of his circle. Why, you don't think he stole the miniature, do you?'

'Don't worry about what I think,' Blackstone said. 'I just want you to keep your ears open.'

'And what will I be listening for?'

'Rumours. Gossip.'

'I should have to be more discriminating than that. All I ever hear is rumour and gossip. What do you want, Blackstone? Intelligence on Cumberland's intentions towards the Princess? Because that's the real reason you're here, isn't it?'

'Something like that. But if you let one word slip about what I'm asking you to do I'll have every town crier in the land proclaiming your debts.'

'Very well.' He stood up. 'If my intelligence is good you will pay me?'

Blackstone, who was 6 ft 2 ins, stood up; but Charlston looked down on him. 'What would be the use? – you'd only lose it on slow horses.'

46

Chapter Five

———————•⚓•———————

BLACKSTONE'S horse, Poacher, was at the far end of the stables. When he saw Blackstone approaching he whinnied and pawed the ground. Blackstone stroked his black coat and checked that he was being well cared for by the Palace grooms.

He was just leaving when one of the grooms came in. Aged about twenty with a thickly-featured face and a lot of muscle bulging his clothes.

The groom said: 'Hey, what the hell do you think you're doing here?'

Blackstone said: 'That's my horse.'

'You haven't any right here.'

'Don't be stupid,' Blackstone said.

He tried to walk out but the groom stopped him.

Blackstone said: 'Take your hands off me.'

But the groom held his coat.

'All right,' Blackstone said quietly. He hit him just below the ribs with his left and, as the groom gasped forward, on the point of the jaw with his right. And then the left into the face again.

The groom settled on the straw-covered floor.

Blackstone waited for him to get up. But he didn't bother. It worried Blackstone that he hadn't tried to fight. Because there was a lot of muscle there.

He worried about it for the rest of the evening.

47

Chapter Six

········

In his room overlooking Kensington Gardens Blackstone checked his luggage to see if it had been disturbed; but the gossamer of black silk around the lock was unbroken.

Then he checked his reserve of guns. Elisha Collier's new flintlock with the revolving cylinder, a self-priming pan cover and the tapered barrel. The two old tap-actioned pocket pistols lying cosily beside each other in the green baize bed of their case. A four-barrelled duck's foot pistol for firing into mobs in confined spaces. A couple of pocket pistols by Joseph Manton.

Then he took off his jacket, lay down on the bed and rang for tea. Outside wind and rain hustled away the memory of summer and pressed the smoke from the chimneys low across the courtyards. A dog barked, a clock chimed.

The housemaid hovered uncertainly. Her hair beneath her bobbinet cap was in springs of curls, fresh from papers, her breasts as playful as puppies beneath her black uniform.

But she didn't know what to make of him. One of them or one of us? And why had he got his jacket off? Because if he was one of those who expected liberties then she was off.

'Don't look so worried,' he said.

She bobbed up and down but smiled, servility beginning to lose the battle. 'I'm not worried, sir. Can I get you something?'

'You're wondering whether I'm the sort who will get you dismissed if you're too familiar or dismissed if you're not familiar enough. Isn't that right?'

She said it was and added that her name was Amy Hucklestone.

'Then fetch me a pot of tea, Amy,' he said. 'And make sure
you bring it back yourself.'

She started to curtsey, then cancelled it.

While she was gone he picked up a book called *Domestic
Management or the Art of Conducting a Family*. It advised employers not to allow a manservant to help the maid make the
beds – 'A buxom wench has been known to ask a favourite
footman to assist her and the request has been attended with
bad consequences for herself.'

In another book he found a list of the housemaid's duties.
Lighting the kitchen fire, cleaning the other grates, sweeping
the hall stairs and outside steps and polishing the knocker,
lighting dressing-room fires, emptying chamber-pots, making
the beds (without the assistance of a manservant), cleaning out
the bird-cage, answering the door in a clean apron, mending
linen, ringing bells for dinner, folding down the beds, filling
the warming-pans with hot coals sprinkled with salt to counter
sulphurous fumes. The result of too much kneeling was pre-
patellar bursitis and the cures were said to be rest or surgery.
An under-housemaid was paid about fourteen guineas a year.

Poor little drudge, Blackstone thought as she returned with
the tea. He pointed to a chair. 'Sit down and put your feet
up.'

'I couldn't,' she said, sitting down.

'I suppose you know what this is all about?'

'Someone's helped themselves to the Princess's miniature.'

'And you're the only member of the staff I haven't interviewed.'

'Well, I haven't done nothing.'

'I'm sure you haven't. Here, have a cup of tea. We'll share
the cup.' He handed it to her, noticing that a faint bloom of
rouge had appeared on her cheeks since she went for the tea.

He put his stock questions to her, then asked: 'Where do
you come from, Amy?'

'The slums,' she said.

'Which ones? There are a lot of them.'

'Holborn.'

'I was born there.'

'You weren't!' She looked at him with surprise and he was pleased. 'You've done well for yourself, then.'

'You're doing all right, Amy.' (Better, at least, than most of the girls from the Rookery who went on the street at fourteen – or younger – and ended up with the pox.)

'Me? The best I can hope for is to marry a footman and have his children.'

They stared out at the London rain and knew that what she said was true; that birthright was decisive; that there weren't too many fairy godmothers around to change it. He felt a sharing between them and wondered if she did too.

So he changed direction. 'How do you get on with the Germans here?'

'All right. I never did take much to foreigners. I've never spoken to the Duchess, of course. Nor to either of the Princesses. But Fräulein Lehzen seems all right according to all accounts. Hannah the nursery maid says she's all right but a bit too particular about Princess Drina. You know, making sure she doesn't have any laudanum or anything like that.'

'Laudanum?' Blackstone sat up on the bed. 'Why should she have laudanum?'

Amy Hucklestone was pleased that she had caused surprise. 'To make her sleep at night, of course. Lots of nursemaids use it to keep the children quiet at night so they can enjoy themselves. You ask any pharmacist. They'll tell you how much laudanum they give out of a Saturday evening.' She seemed to remember Blackstone's position. 'Not that I'm saying it's ever been done with Her Highness. Not on your life. And in any case she's too old for that sort of thing now. But the point is that Fräulein Lehzen still checks up to make sure that she isn't getting any of the stuff. She's a mite too particular. . . .'

Blackstone relapsed on the bed, hands behind his neck. 'Laudanum,' he repeated. But it was ridiculous: once again he was treating the business seriously.

Amy sought light relief. 'Do you know what we call Fräulein Lehzen?' she asked.

Blackstone said he didn't.

'Walnut.'

'Why walnut?'

'Because she's got an Adam's apple like a walnut.'

She lingered over her tea and after a while Blackstone asked her about the other servants. In particular about the lady's-maid who concocted the cosmetics and perfumes in the still room and would have poisons at her disposal.

Amy talked freely about the lady's-maid as Blackstone knew she would: he had never met a junior servant who didn't dislike the lady's-maid.

The lady's-maid was called Irma. She was Swiss – a compromise between German and a fashionable French maid – and she was, according to Amy, a gossip and a madam.

Blackstone also asked her about the new footman, Lawler.

To his surprise Amy looked embarrassed. 'He's nice,' she said.

The lecherous chameleon Lawler.

'But is he trustworthy?'

'You couldn't find a more trustworthy man,' she said.

'I hear he had very good references.'

'The best. But he's also very spirited,' she added, as if good references implied dreary rectitude.

'Spirited?'

Amy looked more embarrassed. 'He likes a laugh,' she explained. 'He's a great one for jokes.' She stumbled on. 'I'm just saying he's nice – nothing more. It's such a change to get someone who laughs a lot down there.' She pointed through the floorboards. 'Not that he's particularly attractive or anything. I wouldn't want you to think . . .' The words melted and stopped.

He smiled at her. 'I don't think anything, Amy. I'm asking questions about everyone. Because somewhere in this homely old building there's a thief.'

'And of course it's one of the servants,' she said with spirit.

'Not at all. There's some pretty unsavoury characters around above the stairs at the moment.'

'Yes,' she said, 'there are.' She took an envelope from the silver tea tray. 'I almost forgot. A note from Lady Hatherley.'

Blackstone took the envelope. 'Is she pretty unsavoury?'

'It wouldn't be proper for me to say.'

'Come off it, Amy.'

'She's a bitch.'

He grinned at her and she smiled back, the fellow conspirator.

The note, scrawled with impatience, said she understood that he had been trying to contact her and she would be available at 4pm.

'Let's share another cup of tea,' he said. Outside a wind-ruffled pigeon perched on the window-ledge and peered in at them.

He had checked on Lady Jane Hatherley because all her loyalties should have been with the enemy camp at St James's. Her husband was a soldier and a close friend of Cumberland, himself a favourite of King George. In Court circles today you were either in the St James's camp or in the German camp at Kensington.

St James's had the power, the glory, the King and his corruption. Kensington, commanded by Conroy, had a future Queen. You took your pick: grace and favour now at St James's or a gamble with the indefinite future at Kensington – provided that the Duke of Clarence, the next King, didn't manage to produce another heir.

So what was the Lady Jane from the bosom of King George and 'Uncle Ernest' doing at Kensington? Blackstone presumed that she was either spying for the King and Cumberland or taking the long-term gamble.

But she didn't look like a sycophant. Nor did she blend with the Kensington scene – the worrying Germans and the languid English.

She carried her title in her walk – seeing few people as she swept around the corridors. (Holly at the neck as a child?) She had a pale face and reddish hair; long legs and small breasts beneath her silks.

Blackstone decided to get Lawler to investigate closer.

After Amy Hucklestone had gone he glanced at his watch. It was 3.55pm. He wrote on the back of Lady Jane Hatherley's envelope, 'Sorry, I'm not available today,' and sent it back to her.

Within two hours Lawler had the information, which he brought to Blackstone's room. It had been easy, he said, because a Swiss lady's-maid called Irma had been seconded to Lady Jane. And he had made contact with Irma, he added in his new footman's voice.

Lady Jane, according to Irma, was two people. By day she helped the Duchess prepare the Princess for the time when she would have to appear in Court; by night she reverted to character – or what Irma decided was her true character.

She sang, she drank wine and she had men visitors.

Blackstone felt vaguely disappointed. He asked Lawler how many men visitors she had. Lawler said that in fact Irma could only recall one, Sir Rupert Charlston. When he was there Lady Jane's voice became different, released somehow. And cruel, Irma, who was learning English with the help of 3d novels and ½d love-song sheets, had added.

At least, Blackstone thought when Lawler had gone, he had some ammunition for his interview with Lady Jane. It was a pity that gossip was so infectious because he could already imagine her with Charlston: his heavy assurance and his butcher's legs. He could hear the 'cruelty' in her voice; he had heard this quality before in privileged girls; it wasn't always positive cruelty, merely misdirection as to what you should point and laugh at; sometimes he detected uncertainty in such voices. And loneliness.

The rain had stopped and the dusk dripped. He took some snuff and lay back on the bed. Conscientiously he was doing his job. There *were* intrigues, there *were* schemers. But they were actors assembled on a stage without a play. You could investigate day after day until you had completed the definitive work on Life at Kensington Palace. But there was no justification for it.

He decided to give it one more week. Then Page could take over and catch the butler picking Conroy's pockets. He would go racing, see a prizefight or take a trip on the new railway from Stockton to Darlington, steam and smuts and rails having become a passion of his since he had seen Stephenson's engine 'Active' pull the first public passenger train between those two towns the previous year.

He was still lying there watching the engine's steam losing itself in a blue winter sky when Conroy summoned him to his room to tell him that the miniature which the King had given the Princess really *was* missing.

Chapter Seven

※

THEY walked together one hundred yards behind the main party clustered around the Princess and Conroy's daughter, Victoire, who were taking turns in riding a pony with blue ribbons on its harness.

Jane Hatherley was dressed in a grey coat over a lighter grey dress that whispered as she walked, reminding Blackstone of the long legs beneath it. She carried a parasol which he thought looked incongruous on a damp cold day with the leaves pasted to the ground. There were a few predatory soldiers around, and some children flying kites which looked as if they might vanish in the low sky.

She said: 'You should have come to see me when I asked you yesterday.' There was a bloom of breeding to her voice; but she looked around her as if she were hardly aware of the outside world.

'I had other things to do.'

'Really. Better things?'

'No, just other things.'

'I understand you want to see me because the Princess's miniature is missing.'

Which was now partly true. He had a plot of sorts.

'I think that's an impertinence,' she told him.

'You're not alone in thinking that. I've questioned everyone. Even the butler.'

'Has it occured to you that the Princess may have lost it?'

'Hardly.' With some relief Blackstone realized that he could now supply details of the theft. 'One of the Germans put it in a jewel box in a changing room next to the Princess's nursery and locked it. The jewel box was forced open.'

'And how do you think I can help you?'

'The way everyone else has been helping. By telling me about their servants, by telling me about anything suspicious they may have noticed.'

'The only suspicious person I've noticed is you snooping around the Palace. Do you know something?' She stopped and they stared at each other. 'I don't think you came here to investigate the theft of the miniature at all.'

'Why do you think that?'

'I don't know. It's difficult to say. Until today I didn't believe the miniature had been stolen. There didn't seem to be enough urgency about anything.'

'The Duchess of Kent didn't want word to reach the King that the miniature had been lost. There's enough bad blood between the two of them as it is.'

'I suppose so. But the questions you've been asking . . . they didn't seem to tie up somehow. Anyway' – she turned and began to walk again – 'I can't help you with anything. So I suggest we catch the others up.'

He put his hand on her arm; she tried to shake it off but it stayed. 'What are you doing at the Palace?' he asked.

'You know what I'm doing. The Duchess thinks the Princess should have some glimpse of what her future life will be like. Although of course she won't be told for a long time that she will probably be Queen. I'm helping to prepare the way. A little extra tuition beyond what her Governess, the Duchess of Northumberland, will teach her. Now please take your hand off my arm.'

'But why you? I should have thought you were the last person to have got the job.'

'Why, because of Cumberland?' She smiled for the first time that morning. 'Poor old Ernest Augustus. He's not as bad as he's painted.'

'It depends on your standards,' Blackstone said. 'He did cut his valet's throat. But perhaps that sort of behaviour is usual at the Court of St James.'

'Thirteen years ago,' Jane Hatherley said, 'a man called Henry White was gaoled for fifteen months for making the same slanderous accusation.'

'Maybe. But the fact remains that the faithful valet Sellis did have his throat slit.'

'You would have thought,' she said, 'that someone with your knowledge of crime would get his facts straight. The Duke was found in his apartments at St James's Palace with a head wound. Sellis was found with his throat cut. The explanation was that he had attacked the Duke and cut his own throat because he had failed.'

'Mmmm. And the Duchess of Cumberland. Isn't she reputed to have murdered her two previous husbands?'

'You repeat gossip as if it were truth. Not much of a recommendation for a policeman.'

'I don't think the Catholics feel very sorry for him. He is, I believe, Grandmaster of the Orangemen.'

'Really?'

Blackstone felt that she didn't know too much about Catholics seeking emancipation or Protestant hostility to their aims. Or perhaps anything outside Court circles. She glanced, with vague curiosity, at the commoners walking on the grass speckled with seagulls like traces of melting snow.

Blackstone said: 'You haven't answered my question. Why you? Even if Cumberland isn't as villainous as he's painted it doesn't alter the fact that the Duchess of Kent hates him. So why you, Lady Jane?'

'For heaven's sake,' she said, 'who says the Duchess hates Cumberland?'

'The Duchess,' Blackstone said.

The procession proceeded more briskly than usual, towards Apsley House, the usual limit of the walk. At one of the entrances to the Gardens they paused while Victoire Conroy got off the pony and the Princess mounted.

At the far end of the entrance Blackstone noticed a shabby black carriage waiting. A man was strolling towards it.

'I think we'll join the others,' Jane Hatherley said. 'Or at least I will. I presume you have to keep your place back here.'

Blackstone grinned: there was nothing else for it. 'You'll stay with me for a while.'

'I won't, Mr Blackstone.' The divine right – but a little shaky.

'You'll do what I say.'

'And you'll be dismissed as soon as we get back to the Palace.'

'One of us will,' Blackstone said. 'But first tell me about Sir Rupert Charlston.'

She stopped again and looked at him with disgust. The commoner intruding into privileged cloisters set aside by pedigree.

'What about him?'

'What's he been doing in your rooms at night? That's a good enough place to start.'

When he saw the shock in her face he almost felt sorry for her. Almost.

But there was a diversion. A large water dog wandered in between the legs of the pony. The pony bolted with the Princess hanging on to its neck.

There were Germanic shouts of horror and the two footmen started after it. One of them was the new man, Lawler, now called John.

The pony headed for Blackstone and Jane Hatherley. It looked more boisterous than terrified, as if it were happy to have found an excuse to escape.

As it galloped past Blackstone grabbed the reins. He dropped his baton and lost his hat before the pony stopped.

The Duchess, the Lady-in-Waiting, Fräulein Späth, and Fräulein Lehzen rushed up patting and hugging the Princess tearfully. After a few moments of this she broke loose and said: 'Thank you, Blackstone. You were very brave.'

The hysteria died down, the Duchess of Kent thanked Blackstone. The calmest person had been the Princess.

The Duchess said: 'And now we must get straight back to the Palace. The Princess must have an early night to recover from the shock.'

'But I wasn't shocked, mama.'

Fräulein Lehzen straightened the Princess's straw hat. 'Mama knows what's best,' she said.

The Princess looked at Blackstone. He smiled at her and extended his hands. 'What do you think, Blackstone? Am I shocked?'

'You certainly don't look shocked, Your Highness. You acted very sensibly. But,' he added diplomatically, 'I'm sure your mother knows best.'

The Princess paraphrased him. 'You see, Blackstone says I'm all right.'

'We are very grateful to you,' the Duchess said.

The two Fräuleins patted his arm.

The Princess announced: 'I always want Blackstone near me.'

Fräulein Lehzen said: 'Perhaps Mr Blackstone would not want that.'

Princess Alexandrina Victoria looked at her in surprise. What had that got to do with it?, her expression implied.

John the footman took the pony and the party headed back to Kensington Palace.

Blackstone turned to Jane Hatherley. 'Now,' he said, 'I wonder which of us would be dismissed if it came to a trial of strength.'

'Such bravery,' Jane Hatherley remarked. 'A pony arrested by a Bow Street Runner.'

Her room faced the orangery. It was a brownish room, excessively neat, with spindly furniture, a red-cushioned couch, some leather-bound books that looked valuable and boring, a vase of expiring chrysanthemums, a portrait by William Fowler of some morose aristocrat who had posed with the toothache. Hardly the chamber for midnight orgies.

'You see,' she said, 'this is where everything happens. This is where Sir Rupert visits me. And incidentally where *you* shouldn't be visiting me.'

'You could tell me to leave.'

'And have you sneaking to the Duchess? Telling her that I'm refusing to co-operate in preventing anything happening to her daughter? Not likely, Mr Blackstone.'

Blackstone sat down on the sofa and considered her naïvety; that at least was refreshing. 'Who said anything about anything happening to the Princess?'

She made a business of rearranging the chrysanthemums, which should have been on a neglected grave. 'I thought you did. Perhaps not. I suppose I presumed too much because the Princess's miniature had been stolen.'

'You seemed to think it was merely missing.'

'Missing then. Or perhaps I heard some gossip from the servants. This girl Irma spreads every rumour she can lay her tongue on.'

'Not only Irma,' Blackstone said. 'I think someone else told you that the Princess was in danger. Who was it?'

She didn't tell him and he didn't press it because he knew already. He listened instead to her voice as she tried to escape from her own trap. A honeyed voice, with coarse sugary grains sticking in her throat. There was a repressed quality about it. A fanatic or actress or wanton imprisoned by breeding.

'You're not listening to what I'm saying.'

'I was listening to your voice.'

'And what's that supposed to mean?'

'Just that.' He looked at the crystal decanter and glasses on the weak little table. 'Perhaps we could have a glass of wine?'

'You think I have a cellar here and carouse all night with Sir Rupert?'

'Now why should I think that?' he asked gently. His appetite for questioning was fading; it was too easy. But she thought she was astute and that was nice.

'What about some wine?' he repeated.

'I'll ring for some.'

They each drank a glass of claret brought by a footman called Charles, which was probably not his real name.

He watched her drink the next glass, with a touch of defiance as if she wanted to uphold a reputation.

'So, tell me why you receive Sir Rupert here?'

'He's a friend of the family.' She paused, holding the wine in her mouth for a moment. 'A friend of my husband's. My husband,' she explained, 'is away at the moment. He's a soldier and he's in Russia. We've signed a treaty, haven't we? Before that he was fighting in Burma. Not very edifying. In fact,' she said, 'I hardly ever see my husband.'

'I presume it was Charlston who told you about the fears for the Princess's safety?'

'You change the subject very quickly, Mr Blackstone.'

'Part of the art of questioning.'

'I'm sure you're very adept at that art.'

'Not bad.'

'You don't seem to be doing very well at the moment.'

He grinned. 'You really don't think so, do you?' He poured more wine for them both.

She said: 'I see you carry a gun,' and looked pleased with herself.

He took out the pocket pistol with his initials inlaid on the silver behind the firing mechanism. He had found that women liked to see guns; there was some sort of association there.

'Do you think Cumberland has designs on the throne?' he asked.

'I doubt it,' she said.

'He's pretty near to the throne. Let's assume George is going to die soon. A fair assumption, the way he's living. Then we have dear William. If he dies without any more children Drina will become Queen. Which means that there's only Drina standing between Cumberland and the throne.'

'Poor Uncle Ernest. Can you imagine a one-eyed, scar-faced monarch on the throne?'

'We couldn't do much worse than we're doing now.'

'I don't believe any of these rumours about Cumberland,' she said.

'You sound as if you're trying to convince yourself.' He topped up her glass. 'Have you heard anything specific?'

'So you're not really interested in the disappearance of the miniature.'

'Have you heard anything?'

'If I had I wouldn't tell you, Mr Bow Street Runner.'

Blackstone acknowledged the work of alcohol. Stoking up her loyalties and simultaneously oiling indiscretion. He wondered how it affected her physical resistance.

She said: 'I've read about you, Edmund Blackstone.' He poured another dribble of claret into her glass. 'Weren't you involved in that Cato Street affair?'

'I was,' he said. 'In a minor way.'

'And you've been involved in quite a few escapades since.'

Blackstone said there had been a few.

'And you think you're very important, don't you?'

Blackstone said he didn't.

She leaned back in her chair. 'Big and handsome in a common sort of way. As conceited as hell. And too damned sure of yourself.'

'That sounds a fair description,' Blackstone agreed.

'Do you like music?'

'Up to a point.'

'What are your interests then, Mr Blackstone? Apart from arresting people and beating them and getting paid for it.'

Blackstone shrugged. 'You wouldn't appreciate my interests.'

'Try me.'

'Cricket.'

'No,' she said.

'Prizefighting.'

'That's illegal.'

'Women.'

'Absolutely not.'

'Railways.'

'Just possibly,' she said.

'Gambling?'

'Quite probably if it were considered ladylike. Trains and gambling. Maybe. . . . You know,' she said, sipping her claret, 'you're the first man apart from servants I've really spoken to outside Court circles.'

'I'm honoured.'

'Don't be sarcastic. You're not honoured at all. But I sometimes wonder if I would enjoy life outside . . .'

'But not enough to find out.'

'It's difficult,' she said. She fingered the ringlets that fell away from her precise middle parting.

'Nonsense,' Blackstone said. 'You could find out if you wanted to. Take a walk round the Rookery one night. Go for a whitebait dinner on Greenwich waterfront. Ask Charlston to buy you a drink in the Shades in St Martin's Lane. Go down to Snow Hill and Limehouse . . .'

'Surely,' she said, 'it's possible to find out what life's like outside St James's and Kensington without going to those extremes.'

'What makes you think they're extremes?'

'The way you talk about them. The sarcasm in your voice.' She picked up her glass but put it down again without drinking. 'You know, Mr Blackstone, you are quite common, aren't you?'

He looked at his Breguet 18ct quarter repeater watch given to him by a very satisfied client. 'I presume it's Sir Rupert's turn now?'

She threw the claret. Most of it splashed over his face, the rest spattered his glistening white shirt-front with the fluted frill down the middle.

'Such a waste,' he said.

Chapter Eight

In the footmen's public house, a hundred yards down the road from the butler's tavern, Lawler prepared his oral report for Blackstone. It was difficult, because the servants' hall was a warren of intrigue. And you couldn't always tell which intrigues mattered, which would interest Blackstone. There was intrigue recounted from above by lady's-maids and valets – when they had drunk sufficient gin; there was intrigue among themselves, about the housekeeper and the butler, the maid and the groom. Any of it might have significance which only Blackstone would spot.

Blackstone had told him to get as close to the Princess as possible. Easy. Because he had been assigned to the head nurse under Fräulein Lehzen, the German successor to Mrs Brock. And the head nurse whose name was Mary Singleton had taken a fancy to him.

He waited in the corridor while the Princess was dressed and undressed as many times as a doll; he accompanied the party on their walks through Kensington Gardens to Apsley House: once he went down to Claremont when the Princess was visiting her Uncle Leopold, of whom she was very fond.

He watched and he listened and he heard very little.

In his room between ten o'clock and twelve at night he was visited by Mary Singleton who fed him with biscuits coated with hard pink and green icing-sugar and told him how honoured he should be because she had never imagined herself consorting with anyone less than a butler.

'There you are,' Lawler said. 'You never know your luck.'

She wasn't very attractive, he thought, with her heavy chin and her greedy eyes. He had courted a nurse once; but she had been a wet nurse and had given him much comfort, including some of the generous ration of stout that she was allowed every day.

It was part of Mary Singleton's duties to safeguard the Princess against danger. To make sure that rivers and ponds were fenced, to check fire precautions and, when the Princess was younger, to fix up a rope with a sack on the end in which to lower the Princess to the ground in the event of an emergency.

'Have you noticed anyone suspicious hanging about?' Lawler asked, refusing a biscuit.

'No. No one. Except that you begin to imagine things the way Fräulein Lehzen carries on.'

'The Princess is very fond of her.'

'She's all right, I suppose.' Her tongue searched for crumbs on her lips. 'She'd do anything for Drina,' she added grudgingly. She patted the edge of Lawler's bed. 'Why don't you come and sit down here? I won't bite you.' She looked as if she would.

Later she said: 'You know, John, I could get you dismissed any time I wanted to.'

'But you wouldn't want to, would you?' He looked in the mottled mirror and thought how white and under-fed his body looked.

'I'm not saying I would. I'm just telling you that I could.' She covered her bosom in the aggrieved way that some women have after they've made love. She said: 'I wouldn't want to think that you were running after any other women servants, John.'

Lawler thought about Amy Hucklestone. 'I wouldn't do that,' he said.

'I thought you might have eyes for that Swiss miss, Irma.'

Lawler was relieved. 'I've hardly even noticed her,' he said. 'On my life.'

It was next day that Blackstone told him to cultivate Irma.

He found her in the still-room fiddling about with her lotions, powders and ointments. He flirted with her which was not quite permissible. Lady's-maid or housekeeper with the butler. Nursemaids and housemaids with the footmen. Kitchen maids and dairy maids with grooms and under-gardeners.

She let this be known.

But he persisted, asking her what she was doing.

She was proud of her accomplishments and she told him that she was making alum water. He picked up the book beside her but he couldn't read very well. 'What do you have to do?' he asked.

She listed the ingredients: calves' feet chopped up, melons, cucumbers, fresh eggs, lemons, skimmed milk, rose water, the juice of water lilies, some wild tansy and half an ounce of borax.

All this in thick chocolate accents. 'And then you distil it,' she said.

'Do you ever use any laudanum?' he asked, remembering one of Blackstone's requests.

She looked surprised. 'I don't use it. But there is some here. Left by some of the visitors' nursemaids, I expect. They use it to keep the babies quiet.'

'I know,' Lawler said. 'Sometimes they're so quiet you never hear another peep out of them.'

'You mean they die?'

Lawler nodded.

'That's terrible.'

'You're a very sensitive girl,' he told her.

She looked pleased, but in a way that indicated she was accustomed to compliments. He put his arm round her waist and she removed it, but gently.

He said: 'Have you ever noticed if any laudanum's missing?'

She shook her head.

'Keep an eye open for me,' he said.

Her pretty, dairy-fresh face looked puzzled. 'Why should I do that?'

'Because it's poison,' Lawler told her. 'Just like that bottle of mercury there. What do you use that for?'

66

Irma told him that it was for removing tight rings from ladies' fingers. You touched the ring with the mercury and gave it a slight blow with a hammer; this broke the ring.

'What happens to the ring then?'

'Whatever the lady decides.'

'Which means you keep it and sell it?'

Irma tried to look dignified, a difficult role for a plump and flirtatious girl. 'You don't sound like a proper footman to me,' she said.

'Why not?'

'I don't think you can even read,' Irma said. 'All footmen should be able to read and write.'

'I didn't know that,' Lawler told her. He put his arm round her waist again but she knocked it away. He shrugged. 'I want you to do something for me, Irma. I want you to keep your eyes and ears open. I want you to keep an eye on that laudanum. I want you to report anything suspicious to me. And in particular I want you to help me find that miniature because I don't think it ever left the Palace.'

She put her hand to her plump cheek with theatrical outrage. 'How dare you ask me to do things like that. I shall go and see the housekeeper this instant and tell her that you're not a footman at all and that most probably you know something about that miniature and you're trying to hide it with all this talk about suspicions. . . .'

Lawler let her ramble on a bit. Then he said: 'If you do I'll tell the housekeeper that you're no more Swiss than a Welsh rarebit and then we'll both be out of a job.'

Lawler also got friendly with some of the other men servants lowly enough to eat and drink ale with him, and a few more women servants. The cook was stubbornly opposed to co-operation until he caught her paying her liquor bill with two silver spoons marked with a German coat-of-arms.

But no one knew anything about the miniature.

Lawler despised most of the servants, the men anyway, because of their servility – although he conceded that they hadn't much choice. He supposed he just didn't like servants.

But he did like Amy Hucklestone. And they often talked about their lives in the slums of Holborn. 'That Mr Blackstone comes from Holborn,' she told him one evening. 'You'd never believe it, would you?' Lawler said he wouldn't.

Their friendship developed and, although he preferred her company to that of anyone else, he didn't touch her. He wasn't sure why. There was about her a quality which he hadn't encountered anywhere else. He had an unpleasant feeling it was honesty.

He drank his ale and, with the negative report rehearsed, went down the road to the coffee house where he had arranged to meet Blackstone. He wondered how business was in the Rookery; and in the places where betting men meet. They wouldn't miss him, he knew; and they would accept him back when all this was over as if he hadn't been away. Perhaps some of his creditors clamouring to be paid might have quietened down by the time he returned: you had to look on the bright side.

Blackstone was spooning brown sugar into his coffee, looking better dressed than any other man in the place. Seeing him sitting there you wouldn't realize what a hard bastard he was, Lawler thought. Unless you paused to take in the width of shoulder and the thickness of wrist, unless you noticed certain lines on his face. Lawler knew all about those lines: they were to be found on the faces of men who had starved as children before earning enough money to put on flesh. The lines could never be erased.

Blackstone had put his baton away to avoid embarrassing Lawler. But he needn't have worried – no one knew Lawler in Fulham. Chelsea, perhaps, where cleaned-out gamblers with style managed to eat oysters on credit. But not respectable Fulham.

Blackstone greeted him without enthusiasm. Lawler suspected that he had no appetite for the job either.

Lawler reported his lack of progress. Blackstone nodded as

if it confirmed his own beliefs. Lawler attempted to duck inside the aura of friendship created by their shared misfortunes. 'It seems a hell of a waste of time and money,' he said.

Blackstone said: 'Don't worry, you'll be paid.'

Lawler nodded. 'I know I will,' he said, ducking outside the aura once again.

Chapter Nine

⁕

SIR Richard Birnie considered the complaint about Blackstone in his office: it wasn't the first, but it was the most painstaking. Written by a lawyer and signed or marked by half a dozen villains.

The complainant was a groom from Kensington Palace alleging that Blackstone had brutally assaulted him. He had statements from two coachmen as witnesses and testimony from a physician that his sight had been affected by the blow. The sympathizers who attested with crosses or wandering signatures claimed that at various times they, too, had been assaulted by Blackstone.

The lawyer demanded that Blackstone should be charged. Failing that he should be sacked. If neither was done then the complaint would be published in the *Morning Herald*.

Which would delight Peel, Birnie thought, staring down the elegant street curving like a priest's collar around the squalor of Covent Garden. Peel, the conniving crusader who wanted to establish a police force against the wish of the people. Throughout history the British people had resisted this. Pitt had tried, Cromwell had tried; but the hatred of the British against uniformed interference in their freedom had beaten them.

But Peel was more cunning. Cunning and self-righteous, a dangerous combination. Birnie had no doubt that the gaudy Foot Patrol established four years ago was intended by Peel as the vanguard of an overall metropolitan force, disguised as an enlargement of Bow Street.

Birnie ordered tea and lit his long clay pipe.

What the hell was Peel about? The history of Bow Street was one of enlightened progress. The horse patrols which had driven the highwaymen from the approaches to London, the ordinary foot patrols which had done battle with the footpads, the Runners recognized throughout the world as the élite of detectives.

The people didn't want another force. But what did their wishes matter when a politician was launched on a crusade?

Devoutly, Sir Richard Birnie from Banff, former saddle-maker with Macintosh and Co. in the Haymarket, wished that Peel would stick to his other reforms, if reforms there had to be. (Birnie tended to the Duke of Wellington's view that change could only be for the worse.) Although he acknowledged that the banishing of the death sentence for many felonies, the removal of obsolete laws and the outlawing of man-traps to catch poachers were necessary. Sir Richard was not an unkind man: merely just, very just.

Now some of his men were playing straight into the hands of the committees nosing into the affairs of the Bow Street Runners, the watchmen, the parish constables – even the magistrates. Mixing with the scum of the underworld, acting as messengers between robbers and victims, taking the law into their own hands.

Runners like Blackstone.

And he had gone too far.

Birnie picked up the file on Blackstone and read extracts with regret. An affinity between the two men breathed from the pages; the musk of a man who, like himself, had crossed the class boundary, a border as closely guarded as the limits of the Tower.

Birnie relit his pipe from the fire and thought a little guiltily about his rented house in St Martin's, his cottage at Acton, his wife, the daughter of a rich baker, who, with the present King, had helped him make the crossing.

He turned the pages. No doubt about the bravery of the man. Defying corrupt magistrates of the Cinque Ports who were in league with the smugglers, fighting with a highwayman on a rooftop near Finchley Common, diving into the Thames to rescue a fourteen-year-old pregnant girl trying to commit suicide.

Birnie remembered Blackstone's first job as a Runner. The Cato Street Conspiracy as it became called. He himself had been in charge of it, sixty years old and assistant magistrate. They had decided not to wait for the Coldstream Guards and Ruthven had gone in first followed immediately by Blackstone. Blackstone had fought the cut-throats in the Marylebone stable like a madman, tossing away his used pistols, and hacking into the mob with a stiletto. After the second attack, when the Guards had arrived, the mob's leader, Thistlewood, had escaped only to be recaptured that night. Another man, Henry Challoner, had also escaped: Blackstone had chased him until loss of blood from a thigh wound had stopped him.

But bravery and commendations weren't enough. Not these dangerous days when politicians listened as attentively to the word of a crooked pawnbroker as they did to a magistrate.

God knows, Birnie thought, he had been indulgent with the Runners. He had tried to forget what he knew of their less publicized methods and contacts; he had rarely questioned items charged as payments to contacts – and had never asked who the contacts were. In Blackstone's case he had also ignored the vague suggestions of immorality that surfaced from time to time.

You couldn't ignore the occasional allegations of confessions extracted under duress, i.e. beating a prisoner where he didn't bruise until he admitted his guilt. And, although Blackstone had always cleared himself, Birnie had been forced to warn him about over-zealousness. That's why he'd given him the nursemaid job. And because he was one of the best men he had.

Now this. Birnie looked with distaste at the complaint, made even more unsavoury by a blob of candle-grease on one corner. He saw it in the *Morning Herald*: he saw the satisfaction on the face of Peel.

He shook his head sadly and called for a messenger to go to Kensington to fetch Blackstone.

Blackstone would have to be suspended.

Blackstone wore a brown double-breasted coat with broad velvet lapels and a roll collar. His boots from Hoby's were made of the softest leather and his tall hat had a brim that curved in a sneer. He dressed well, too well for Birnie, whose tastes had been moulded by the sartorial habits of men working with oats, barley and fish. Such elegance gave the critics more ammunition. Where did the money come from for such clothes? A Breguet watch of all things. Certainly not on his meagre salary or his reward money. Everyone knew that Bow Street Runners were paid handsomely by private hirers; but the accusers made such payments sound corrupt.

Birnie indicated a chair opposite his desk. Blackstone took off his coat, sat down and took a pinch of snuff. Birnie tossed the complaint on the desk. 'Read it,' he said.

Blackstone read with the Fieldings, de Veil and Saunders Welch peering over his shoulder.

'Well?'

Blackstone shrugged: his respect had always seemed suspect. But sometimes, in cold moments before sleep, Birnie wondered if he himself hadn't been too respectful in his search for respectability.

Blackstone said: 'It's not the first one of these we've seen, sir.'

'It's the most serious.' He handed Blackstone the accompanying letter threatening publication in the *Herald*.

'And you think Peel and the do-gooders would use it?'

'I'm damn sure they would.'

Blackstone thought it over. 'So what do you want me to do, sir?'

'This isn't the first time this has happened. There was that incident more recently of that man living off immoral earnings. . . .'

'And it won't be the last.'

'I've warned you many times before, Blackstone. You can't

73

go around beating people just because they won't co-operate with you.'

'You are really serious about this one, sir?'

Birnie said he was.

'I don't make a habit of beating people.' He put away the body-smooth snuff-box. 'What should I do – let them beat me first?'

'Your record is worse than anyone else's.'

'I'm sure it's worse than Page's.'

'I don't want personalities to enter into this, Blackstone. The fact is that there have been more complaints about you than any other Runner.'

'Perhaps because I've made more arrests than any other Runner.' He paused, sharpening his argument. 'Surely the point is that none of the complaints have been upheld.'

Birnie put his elbows on the desk. 'You mean they haven't been upheld by me.'

'What's that supposed to mean, sir?'

'It means that some of them may have had some substance but they failed with the burden of proof. Failed with me, that is.' He went to the window and gazed across the street at the Brown Bear, the branch office of the Runners. 'I've always recognized that it's sometimes necessary to use unorthodox methods. You can't rely on ordinary persuasion with a footpad in Islington. But you go too far, Blackstone.'

'Or do you mean, sir, that Robert Peel goes too far?'

'That will be enough, Blackstone.' But Birnie heard the guilt in his own voice. 'Did you beat this groom?' He combed at his grey sidewhiskers with his fingers. 'And please don't tell me that he fell down the steps or walked into a door.'

'Certainly I hit him. He asked for it.'

'And this was in pursuit of your inquiries?'

'In a way. I was questioning everyone. I believe that's what you advised me to do.'

'What exactly do you mean – *in a way*?'

'The reason I hit him wasn't directly to do with my inquiries. He put his hands on me.'

'Ah. So you hit him so hard that, according to a physician, his sight may be permanently impaired?'

'I don't think I hit him that hard.'

'I shall hold an inquiry, of course.'

'It's hardly necessary. I hit him. That's all there is to it. He's got all the rigged witnesses. I've got no one.'

'You know what this means, don't you?'

Blackstone looked at him with surprise, as if he were only just realizing. 'What does it mean, sir?'

'It means that I shall have to suspend you while the inquiry is carried out.'

'Then you'd better suspend me, sir.'

Birnie sat down and leaned across the desk. 'I've always let you have a pretty free hand, Blackstone. Too free, perhaps, because I've always trusted you. If you've acted outside the letter of the law then I've always believed you did so with the highest motives. I have a great respect for you, Blackstone. I don't want to lose you. It will be a great personal loss both for me and for the Bow Street Runners. God knows, with Peel snapping at our heels, we can't afford to let men like you go.'

Blackstone said: 'You seem to be anticipating the result of the inquiry. And the groom *was* employed by the Duchess of Kent.'

'There are a lot of witnesses,' Birnie said. 'Your record is against you.'

Blackstone glanced at judicial dignity in ink and oils around him. He said: 'To think this is where I learned all about justice. . . .'

Birnie pointed his pipe like a gun. 'Don't start lecturing me, Blackstone.'

'I wonder what he would think about it?' Blackstone pointed at Henry Fielding. 'He started it all, didn't he. And old de Veil there who broke up the Black Boy Gang. I don't think he cared too much about public opinion. If he got into trouble he just read the Riot Act. . . .'

Birnie aimed his pipe again. 'The interview is closed, Blackstone. I don't like this any more than you. The point is that if this complaint is published in the newspapers then very soon Henry Fielding's Bow Street Runners won't exist at all. That's what matters, Blackstone. Far more than you or me.'

'You mean you're giving in to blackmail?'

Birnie said: 'You're suspended, Blackstone. But I'll tell you what I'll do – I won't start the inquiry for a week. This will give you time to assemble any witnesses you can find and any evidence you can dig up. Meanwhile I'll take steps to make sure that the lawyer responsible for this document doesn't publish it until you've had a chance.' He peered at the letter. 'The lawyer's name, in case you're interested, is Benjamin Darnley. He gives an address in Wapping, although I doubt if that means very much.'

'I'll remember that when I'm on the other side again and I need a crooked lawyer.'

'I hope you'll never be on the other side again, Blackstone.'

'Would it help if I saved the life of the future Queen?'

Birnie said: 'You are relieved of your duties at Kensington.'

Blackstone stood up. 'Then you'll have to find someone else to act as nursemaid.'

'That will be attended to.' Birnie began to write a letter.

'I can't imagine anyone else agreeing to do the job.'

'They'll do what they're told.'

'Townsend? Will he do what he's told?'

Birnie put down his quill. 'I've told you, Blackstone, I don't want to see you go. I shouldn't have to say things like that. The others specialize: you're an expert in most kinds of crime because' – he almost smiled – 'you have the previous experience. . . . You're the crime consultant. If you leave then we'll find someone else. Page, probably. Townsend's too concerned with conspiracy in high places, Ruthven's getting old and he's going to leave soon to open his own inn. The others are too busy with their specialities. It would have to be Page. . . .'

'God help you,' Blackstone said. He walked to the door and opened it.

Birnie said: 'It's up to you, Blackstone. If you can't dig

anything up within the week then I'll probably have to take your baton back.'

'Oh no,' Blackstone said. 'I'm sorry. You'll never have that back. No matter what happens you'll never have that back.'

He ran down the stairs, his soft leather boots making little noise.

Birnie returned the gaze of his own predecessors. The Bow Street Runners came first. Didn't they?

He drank one hot gin in the Brown Bear but he had no real taste for alcohol. Not at the moment. Just disgust that the values in the public office of Bow Street, ancestor of all the other public offices where justice was administered, weren't so much different from the values of those who were arraigned.

Ruthven was there with Page and a couple of other Runners. Were they aware of the hypocrisy that existed across the street? Aware that when the politicians beckoned the Runners ran?

He bought a round. One more gin for himself. But its scent was corruption. He saw the vanities of his own respectability, the self-righteousness of his law-enforcement. Wasn't Lawler more honest in his way? An honest criminal.

But why had the groom bothered to make such an indictment? A lawyer and six criminal witnesses. It was ridiculous. He had obviously been approached by someone. But why, for God's sake? Peel wouldn't go to those lengths to discredit the Runners.

And it had happened at Kensington Palace where there was supposed to be a plot. There had certainly been a robbery: a strange theft in which the narrative of his own fiction had been filled in.

And Jane Hatherley's lies.

And the attack outside his home the other night in which a sense of familiarity had been as strong and elusive as a perfume from the past.

And the intrusion of the Cumberland set into the German outpost at Kensington.

77

There was something afoot.

Then he remembered the interview with Birnie. His suspension. But Birnie had given him the name of the crooked lawyer. Tonight he would dive once more into London's underworld: the prospect excited him after the artifices of Kensington. Tonight he would find out about the lawyer called Benjamin Darnley; perhaps he might even find a miniature belonging to Princess Alexandrina Victoria.

Because every trained sense now told him that there was a connection.

He excused himself and walked through the smoky, ginny haze to the door.

The girl was waiting for him.

'Hallo, Blackie,' she said, 'I've missed you. I thought perhaps you didn't want to see me any more. I thought you might have found yourself some titled girl.'

'Now what gave you that idea?'

'You know, Blackie, you can't help overhearing what the others say.'

But they didn't know, he thought.

'Never believe what you overhear.'

'Will you be around later?'

He put his arm round her waist. 'Later. Much later.'

'I'll be waiting for you, Blackie,' she said.

He nodded, gazing up at the window across the road where the silhouette of Sir Richard Birnie could be seen. A tough old bastard. A tough, hypocritical, scared old bastard.

Chapter Ten

❧

BLACKSTONE went first to a cock-fighting pit in Drury Lane where criminals collected as thickly as the feathers the pecking, strutting birds tore off each other.

It was almost the end of a main. Seven birds a side with a lot of money staked on each match and a fortune on the overall result.

When he arrived the last two birds were fighting on the matting inside the twenty-foot-wide circular enclosure. The air smelled of blood, farmyards and human excitement.

It was a classic match with seven of the birds belonging to the famous trainer-owner Joseph Gilliver from Lincoln and seven belonging to a newcomer whose birds had only fought in churches and churchyards until now.

The newcomer's birds were at least proving their worth: they were three matches all with the main to be decided on this last match. One bird was already blinded in one eye; but it pecked and hacked with its spurs as it had been taught all its life.

The sport didn't appeal to Blackstone. He didn't like the stench of cruelty, the hypocrisy that the ferocious stupidity of two birds was courage.

Beside the ring overlooking the two bloodied antagonists he found a small man in a green, swallow-tail coat with one hand firmly in his pocket as if he were clutching a few hundred guineas, which he probably was.

He greeted Blackstone and said: 'You're a bit late, Blackie, Gilliver's going to win again.'

'And you've backed him, I presume.'

'Who else?'

Blackstone said he wasn't interested in betting on birds butchering each other.

'They enjoy it,' the little man whose name was Spooner said. 'Just like two prizefighters enjoy it.'

His voice had country notes to it, a drop of cider in the vowels. He was a lawyer and for a while his orchard sincerity had impressed the magistrates of Bow Street, St Martin's, Shoreditch, Southwark . . . and the judges of the higher courts. But not for long. So Spooner had turned to gambling, assisted by information from some of his wealthier clients. He was said to have backed Lap-dog, the 50-1 winner of the Derby; but his style of life didn't reflect his winnings – he lived as if he constantly anticipated the return to country poverty.

Gilliver's cock was working on its adversary's other eye. It shook its beak, spraying blood. The newcomer's bird strutted blindly, pecking at nothing. The spectators shouted and waved their hats, gentry and others keeping themselves to themselves.

Spooner asked Blackstone what brought him to the main.

'Information,' Blackstone said. 'About lawyers. Crooked lawyers. You should know all about them.'

'There's enough of them, Blackie.'

'Ever come across one called Benjamin Darnley?'

Spooner thought for a moment, eyes on the ring. 'Can't say I have. Where does he operate?'

'He has an address at Wapping.'

'Then he can't have much class, Blackie. What do you want to know about him?'

'Who he mixes with. Who his clients are. Who would pay him to rig false evidence against me.'

Spooner shook his head. 'All I can do is to send you to a flash tavern where such members of my profession meet to solicit custom. But you probably know it anyway – Sol's Arms on Wych Street, not far from here. Ben Lewis's tavern.'

Blackstone nodded. He knew it more as the haunt of cracksmen and top-class thieves than bent lawyers.

'But why don't you go down to Wapping?' Spooner asked.

'Because he won't be there.'

'Why not?'

Because, Blackstone thought, he won't be sitting in his office patiently waiting for the same treatment that the groom had got. But there wasn't any need to enlighten Spooner. 'It doesn't matter,' he said.

In the ring the upstart made a last blind thrust at Gilliver's cock. Spooner shook his head. 'Too much corn meal and not enough raw beef in his diet.'

Gilliver's cock dodged and poised itself for the kill. But the other bird lurched the same way and his steel spur caught Gilliver's bird on the leg. It stumbled and the blinded bird stabbed with its beak, finding the neck. Blood jetted brightly from the punctured artery. Gilliver's bird hopped away, slower and slower. It raised its hackle, showing white feathers.

The shouting stopped. Someone yelled: 'Gillie's bird's shown the white feather.'

Two men from the Gilliver party rushed into the ring. But when they reached their bird it was dead. Its opponent died soon afterwards.

From the look on his face Blackstone judged that Spooner might be returning to the country sooner than he had anticipated.

He went next to a 'soup-shop' in Long Acre where he had sometimes managed to seize stolen plate before it was cooked into unidentifiable chunks of precious metal. The melting was carried out behind a pawnbroker's kept by an old fence called Ruben who had lost his second name along with his good name many years ago.

An oil lamp wavered inside throwing aspen leaves of light on paste jewellery, chipped decanters, assorted cutlery, gilt-framed mirrors, a rusty gun or two for explosive suicide. A French hobby-horse, a saddle, a plaster sphinx and a stuffed owl.

Blackstone approached carefully along a side-street to dodge the watchman Ruben employed as a look-out. But if the look-out was anything like the pensioners, cripples and drunks employed as watchmen all over London he didn't have much to worry about.

The look-out was leaning against a cast-iron street lavatory. A bottle protruded from one pocket, but he wasn't drunk. Blackstone took him from behind, clapping his hand over the man's mouth. The look-out struggled, but he was ageing and not very strong. Blackstone told him to keep quiet and released him.

Then he kicked open the door of the shop. It swung open ringing a carillon of cracked bells. Behind the counter old Ruben leapt to his feet shouting in fear and surprise. By which time Blackstone had kicked down the second door and was along the corridor to the third and last. But it was locked. He put his pocket pistol to it and fired. The door swung open.

Beyond it was a cobbled yard and a shed with a crucible steaming inside it. Three men were escaping over a high wall. Blackstone caught one by his boots and pulled him down. As he fell a silver candlestick dropped from his coat.

The man fought briefly, swearing and kicking. Blackstone stood back, cocked the pistol and said: 'Keep still or I'll blow your head off.'

The man lay still.

Old Ruben emerged, breath indignant on the cold night air. He had no idea, he told Blackstone, that villains were using his premises – they must have come over the wall.

Quite pleasantly Blackstone told him to be quiet.

He picked up the candlestick and examined it. 'The Travellers' Club in Pall Mall?'

The thief who was now sitting up didn't reply.

'I asked you a question.'

The thief said: 'I don't know nothing about it.'

Blackstone peered at him. 'Charlie Cranston no less. I didn't know you'd been released from Newgate. I don't give much for your chances, Charlie, if you come up in front of certain judges for this one. There's one or two of them belonging to the Travellers' and they don't like their best plate being pinched.'

Old Ruben said: 'I knew nothing about it. God blind me, I didn't.'

'Perhaps you didn't,' Blackstone said. 'Perhaps you didn't.'

The fence looked surprised.

Blackstone said to Cranston: 'I'm not all that interested in reclaiming candlesticks stolen from the Travellers'.'

The thief looked astonished.

Blackstone explained that he would believe the fence knew nothing about the melting, and that Cranston was on his way to return the candlestick to the Travellers' Club, if they could help him trace a certain miniature set in diamonds.

Blackstone visited an unlicensed dolly shop, seeking news of the miniature amid the stale heaps of pawned clothes; a twopenny-rope lodging house already packed and snoring; Madame Levi's fancy-house; a tavern where men fought on a platform and customers bet on the result; a yard where men wagered on how many rats a terrier could kill in an hour (a dog called Billy was reputed to have killed a hundred), a pornographic peep show and several flash taverns. He spoke to the pieman in the Rookery, to watchmen, bawds, pickpockets, burglars, a murderer or two, half a dozen beggars and a few barefoot children whom he rewarded with coins and hot potatoes.

He wasn't the most popular customer at Ben Lewis's tavern in Wych Street. But there was respect there if not welcome. As there should be, he thought, pushing his way through the fug, because he had never arrested anyone there. You didn't make trouble in a flash tavern where you knew you could find your customers.

Usually he came to Sol's Arms when he had been asked to guard property; jewellery at a ball or paintings on exhibition. There he delivered his warning to all specialists to keep away: if they didn't it wouldn't take him long to pluck them out of

London's labyrinths and charge them with something or other. It usually worked.

He found the cream of the criminal fraternity playing cards and tossing for sovereigns at the far end of the inn. Jack Barclay, the cracksman who drove his own cab with a race-horse between the shafts for escaping, deaf Charlie Brain who commanded an army of pickpockets, Peter Prince the penman who was said to have forged his own pardon in gaol, two or three 'flash gentry' as smartly dressed as Blackstone.

They greeted him without pleasure.

Barclay spoke first. 'Drinks all round landlord – on the Runners.'

Blackstone tossed some coins on the table.

Prince said: 'What are you looking for, Blackie? A pretty little miniature all set in diamonds? I could get a bit-faker to make you one if you like but you'd have to supply the sparkles.'

'News travels fast,' Blackstone said.

'Like wipes out of a rich man's pocket,' Charlie Brain said.

'How would you know? You're supposed to be deaf.'

Brain pointed at his lips. 'There's ways of hearing without listening, Blackie.' He sat back, lips moving as they talked, and then asked: 'How's Mr Page these days, Blackie?'

'He's all right.'

'In for a bit of promotion, maybe?'

'Maybe,' Blackstone said.

Barclay said: 'The word is that you're in trouble, my covey.'

'Who told you that?'

'I think,' Barclay said, 'we'll all have another little wet. On the Runners, of course.'

He was a smart, swaggering man with pearls at his cuffs, black hair brushed forward, Hoby's boots made of leather as soft as Blackstone's.

Blackstone asked again: 'Who told you?'

Prince, whose tongue lied as easily as his pen, said: 'A certain parish constable, Blackie.'

'Don't give me that, Prince.'

Barclay stretched his powerful body, revealing a red and gold waistcoat. 'Don't get too tough, Blackie. You don't make us shake and shiver quite the way you did. How long have they given you? A week?'

'Just supposing they have,' Blackstone said. 'I could do a lot in a week. Have the lot of you behind bars, for instance.'

Barclay thought about it. 'Maybe you could, Blackie. Maybe you could. But I don't think the beak would waste his time with the charges. Not with your reputation as it stands now. You've been a bad boy, Blackie. A very bad boy.' He sipped at his brandy and lit a pipe. 'Word has it that you milled a poor unfortunate groom at Kensington Palace.' He licked his lips. 'There must be some good pickings at the Palace, eh Blackie?'

Blackstone bought them more drinks and waited.

Brain said: 'You've been doing the rounds tonight we hear, Blackie.'

He always managed to *hear* things, Blackstone thought. He said: 'I want some help.'

'So,' Barclay said, 'Edmund Blackstone wants some help.'

Blackstone remembered Barclay's swift grey horse which he nursed like an only child. He leaned forward. 'Do you know why I banged that groom?'

Barclay shook his head.

'Because he was ill-treating a horse.'

'Very touching,' Prince said.

Barclay flicked a speck of ash from the frill of his shirt. 'I must say you've always played it pretty square with us – when it's suited your purpose. What do you want to know, Blackie? Apart from the whereabouts of the miniature. We know it's missing but none of us knows who pinched it.'

'Two things,' Blackstone said. 'First I want to find a crooked lawyer called Darnley. Then I want to know how you came to know about the milling with the groom.'

Barclay pointed at three men sipping hot gin in the corner. They wore dark clothes that had never taken to an iron, and they had about them a watchful air like birds waiting to be fed. 'They'll put you right. They hang around here waiting to take our cases. Brain's hooks or one of Prince's apprentices. Go and have a talk with them.'

Blackstone talked with the frightened lawyers who started to protest in legal terminology. Blackstone listened for a moment. Then he leaned across the table and prodded each below the ribs with his baton. They coughed and gasped for breath, sucking down lungfuls of tobacco smoke as thick as Thames fog. Three not-so-wise owls on a perch. 'Talk,' Blackstone said. They twittered and complained and looked nervously at Blackstone's contacts playing cards in their reserved seats. What did he want to know?, they asked. He explained and they told him what they knew about Darnley and where he might be found. When he returned to the card-players the lawyers looked relieved, huddling together as if to share the heat beneath their moulting feathers.

Barclay bought him a drink and said they'd all been trying to remember who might be behind the complaint to Birnie.

'And did you remember?'

Barclay looked at the others. They nodded. He said: 'The general feeling is that although you're an evil bastard we could get worse if you were thrown out of the Runners. Brain is particularly bothered that we might get Page sniffing around here. *"Take care of your pockets."* Brain wouldn't like that at all.'

'I wouldn't hear him,' said Brain, who seemed to have heard Barclay.

Barclay said: 'Does the name Henry Challoner mean anything to you?'

Five in the morning. He woke from a doze jumbled with plans and theories. He stroked the naked body of the girl from the Brown Bear, her flesh and her fur. She murmured his name and took his hand to her breast, then slept again.

Outside the girl's bedroom window he could see a cold morning star. Henry Challoner. He saw him fleeing down the street, felt the icy sickness as the blood wasted away down his thigh.

But what had Challoner got to do with some cheap conspiracy to get him thrown out of the Runners? It wasn't Challoner's style.

But if Barclay were correct – and he usually was – it was Challoner who had paid the six crooked witnesses to testify against him. So Challoner wanted him out of the way.

Out of the Runners? Or just away from Kensington Palace?

The selection of the groom to start a fight seemed to indicate Kensington. As if Challoner had been following his movements there. But surely Challoner would be concerned in something more ambitious than the theft of the miniature. A theft of which no one in London's underworld seemed to know anything.

He slept again, jerking and crying out as the moonlight found the scar on Challoner's face and it turned to forked lightning. The girl soothed him, saying: 'There, don't be frightened, my love.'

Across the rooftops the October sun rose in flames. He heard the swish of the apprentices' brooms as they watered and brushed the pavements outside the shops: smelled the hot yeast breath of baking bread.

Then if it wasn't the miniature Challoner was after what was it? Assassination was his speciality.

Or kidnap?

He threw back the clothes.

'Blackie,' she said, 'where are you going? What's the time?'

'Half past seven,' he said.

'Come back to bed, Blackie. Just for a little while.' She turned the flap of bedclothes so that he could see her sleepy breasts, her warm loins.

She was right: there wasn't any point in arriving at the Palace too early.

Half an hour later he sat up in bed again, remembering the man who had attacked him in Paddington village. Challoner.

As he dressed, looking at the scrapyard of rooftops, he

wondered why Challoner was so anxious to get rid of him. He would like to think it was fear of his own capabilities.

In a way he respected Challoner. If you could respect a professional killer. Respected not admired. The strength of the man, rising from the slums like a man struggling out of a swamp. In Challoner Blackstone saw a part of himself. The way he might have gone. It was as if they might have had the same father in the great spawning grounds of Holborn.

The girl made tea. She enjoyed this sharing part of the morning as much as the love-making, he thought. Pretending that they would always be together. She reminded him of the maid Amy. The same glimmers of hope against the background of reality, of resignation.

His clothes wore the badges of a night's drinking; his chin was dark. They sipped their tea listening to the cries of London's daily birth.

It occurred to Blackstone as he finished his tea, and the girl poured him more, anxious for him to stay, that although Challoner might want him out of the way because he respected him, there could be a more mundane reason. Challoner wouldn't want to be recognized and hounded through Britain and beyond. He remembered Challoner's slight give-away limp.

He bent and kissed the girl.

She smiled at him. 'Don't worry, Blackie. I mean about Birnie and everything. You'll be all right whatever happens.'

'I wouldn't be too sure,' he said.

'I'll always be here,' she said.

'I know you will,' he said.

He hesitated at the doorway. She was sitting on the edge of the bed holding her cup. She was beginning to cry.

He walked down the winding stairs into the street of old leaning houses where a procession of weavers carrying placards about starvation and living wages was assembling. Then he took a cab to Paddington.

Chapter Eleven

···✠···

THE Princess was ill. Stomach cramps and a slight temperature.
The Duchess, who slept in the same room at night, sat at her
bedside. The doctor sat at the other side. Fräulein Lehzen
worried nearby. Behind her stood the nurse, Mary Singleton;
outside, waiting to run errands, stood John the footman.

After a while the doctor said he thought the Princess's
illness might have been caused by a surfeit of over-ripe pears.
No one believed him.

In his office the Comptroller of the Household, Sir John
Conroy, equerry to the late Duke of Kent, whom he was said
to resemble, received the diagnosis with contempt and ordered
a second opinion. Then he turned his attention to Blackstone.

'You make it very awkward for me,' he said. 'You've been
relieved of your duties here. You can hardly expect me to
allow you to continue your investigations.' He made small
sawing motions with one finger in the deep cleft in his chin –
a habit of his. 'Although I hope that doesn't preclude our
excursion up West one night.'

'You've got to let me stay,' Blackstone said. 'I didn't attach
much importance to the rumours when I arrived. Now I
do.'

'What's changed your mind?'

Blackstone told him about Challoner. 'He wouldn't be so
desperate to get rid of me if there wasn't something big happening. Who knows, it might have been planned for today if
the Princess hadn't fallen ill.'

'Or been poisoned?'

'Surely the doctor would be able to diagnose poison.'

Conroy shrugged. 'I don't have much faith in physicians. They didn't do much for the Duke. They let a chill develop into a high fever which killed him. A good man,' he added staring at the Duke's portrait on the wall. 'Did you know he was connected with sixty-two charitable organizations? I promised him I would do everything in my power to look after his daughter. A gypsy once told him that he would beget a great Queen. That's why he drove like a maniac to Britain so that she could be born on British soil. Delivered here at 4.15 in the morning by the German midwife Fräulein Siebold while the Duke of Wellington and the Archbishop of Canterbury and others waited in another room.'

Blackstone yawned.

'I swore when I saw the baby that I would make sure she reached the throne.'

'Then you'd better let me stay,' Blackstone said.

'I can't. You know that. And let's face it, Blackstone, you haven't produced any results since you came here. There must be someone working on the inside.'

'I've got some ideas.'

'Who?'

Blackstone shook his head thoughtfully. 'Nothing definite. I can't give you any names yet.'

'There's no question of *yet*. You either tell me now or not at all.'

'Then it's not at all,' Blackstone said.

'Are you sure this man Challoner doesn't want to get rid of you because of some private vendetta?'

'He wouldn't go to all this trouble. Let's say we have a healthy respect for each other. No more.' Blackstone wasn't sure if that was quite true. 'But in my opinion he's the most dangerous criminal abroad in London today. And for some reason he wants me out of the way.'

'Because he respects you so much?'

Blackstone shook his head. 'Probably because he thinks I'll recognize him. Not just his face. His walk, his limp, his bearing. And it's also possible that someone believes I'm on to something.'

The maid Amy Hucklestone brought in tea which Conroy took with lemon.

When she had gone Conroy said: 'What do you expect me to do? I can't keep on a Bow Street Runner who's been dismissed.'

'Who said I'd been dismissed?'

'Well, haven't you?'

'I've been taken off this job and suspended pending an inquiry.'

'It amounts to the same thing.' Conroy squeezed the lemon with the teaspoon. 'Before the day's out everyone in the Palace will know if that groom has anything to do with it. You won't have any respect or any authority any more.'

'I've got answers to questions without respect before now.'

'I know – with your fists. You can't do that any more.'

'I could stay on as a guest.'

Conroy looked at him sceptically.

'You don't think I look the part?'

'On the contrary, I think you look too much the part. You dress better than most of the other guests.'

Blackstone's clothes felt suddenly ostentatious.

'I want to stay,' he said.

There was a knock on the door and Amy Hucklestone reappeared. 'There's a gentleman to see you, sir,' she said. 'A Mr Page.'

Conroy sighed with relief. 'You'd better discuss it with your colleague,' he said.

Page said: 'I'm sorry about this, Blackie.'

'Like hell you are.'

'You've never liked me much, have you?'

'No.'

'It's a pity because I've always admired you. Although I knew you looked down on me because I specialized in pickpockets.'

91

Blackstone thought: set a thief to catch a thief. Who was he to talk? But he had always treated Page with contempt because he didn't enhance the name of the Runners. He dealt in petty crime and he extorted money from criminals on a petty scale. Once he had taken a few coins from a pickpocket specializing in robbing theatre crowds on the understanding that he would withhold evidence against him when he came up before Birnie; but he had withheld nothing. Lawler told him this; Page denied it; Blackstone believed Lawler.

They stood in the courtyard near the stables. Blackstone sensed that servants were peering at him and sneering; but it could have been his imagination. Page's hands fluttered nervously over his pockets. His face was pale, his hair and his eyes; he was a biggish man but he gave the impression of being much smaller; because of his role in life, Blackstone decided unkindly.

Blackstone told him that he wanted to stay at the Palace.

That was impossible, Page replied, a sheen of satisfaction in his voice.

'It depends which is more important – your dignity or the safety of the Princess.'

Page thought about it. His dignity obviously. He told Blackstone: 'The future of the Princess comes before everything.'

'Then I'll have to stay.'

Page examined his thin white fingers – a musician's fingers. 'So you think that the Princess's safety depends on you?' He began to enjoy himself. 'You were always conceited, Blackie. You were a good man, I'll grant you that. But not *that* good. You were too crude in your methods. And to be quite honest a lot of people resent your fine clothes and ornaments.'

'Crude, was I?'

'You can't walk over people and get away with it all your life. You've made too many enemies on your way up, Blackie. Now they'll turn on you.'

'Like you?'

'I'm not your enemy. But I've been given this job and I'm

happier because they stopped them from holding public meetings and getting butchered by the yeomanry.'

'But they are much happier. Peel, Huskisson and Canning have seen to that.'

'People are still hungry,' Blackstone said. 'It only needs someone like Wellington to get into power and we'll be right back to 1822. In 1822 we were as near as dammit to our own French Revolution.'

She reined her horse and they stopped beneath a sycamore tree. 'You read a lot,' she said, 'don't you. And you speak very well. . . . '

'For a man with my background?'

'I didn't say that.'

'But you meant it.'

'Tell me about your background,' she said. 'It seems to weigh very heavily on you.' She dismounted and tethered her horse to a branch. 'Tell me about it while we walk.'

The water sucked and gurgled beside them and somewhere in the woods he heard twigs cracking as if someone else were out walking. He stopped. Silence, except for the river and a wood pigeon blundering through the branches.

The sun found a space in the clouds, briefly tossing gold pieces on the water.

She took his arm. 'Your background, Mr Blackstone. Your sinister past. What shall I call you, by the way? I can't call you Edmund – it sounds too grand. It's a bit of a Palace name, isn't it.'

'Blackie will do,' he told her.

'Blackie. I like that. It suits you. What were you before you were a Runner, Blackie?'

'A criminal,' he said.

Her reaction was disappointing. As if she'd always known it.

'What sort of criminal?' she asked.

'All sorts. You name the crime, I committed it.'

'Rape?'

'Never against their will.'

'Murder?'

'Only as an extreme measure.'

'How very disappointing.'

He bent and kissed her. Her lips felt very warm and dry on this cold day. He put one arm round her waist and held her until she responded. Then let her go. 'I also prey on women,' he told her.

'Successfully?' She dabbed her lips with a wisp of handkerchief. She looked as if she wanted to be thought *experienced*; instead she looked uncertain. She said: 'Tell me more about your background. About yourself, Blackie.'

He liked her calling him Blackie.

He told her about the slums. About his two sisters who had died, one from consumption, one from an unspecified fever; in reality both from malnutrition. About the smell of gin permeating their two rooms; about the babies farmed out to the whore next door.

'How did you manage to grow up the way you have?' she asked. 'You aren't exactly a weakling.'

'Survival of the fittest,' Blackstone said.

'Perhaps you take after your father. Was he a big healthy man?'

'I've no idea,' Blackstone told her, watching for reaction again. 'I don't know who he was.'

'I see.'

Because there was so little reaction he pursued it. 'Does that shock you?'

She shook her head. 'But you want it to, don't you?'

Blackstone realized that he did. 'I shouldn't imagine you're accustomed to walking in the woods with bastards.'

She laughed, the honey in her voice grainy. 'You'd be surprised. But tell me about your criminal deeds. That's what interests me, not the fact that you don't know who your father was. For all you know,' she added, 'you might be Royalty. There's enough of their offspring around.'

'I doubt it,' Blackstone said, remembering his mother. 'I'd rather he was a highwayman.'

'Did you pick pockets?'

'Hundreds. I also went into the sewers leading into the Thames looking for valuables. The prize,' he remembered, 'was a ball. Coins collect together and the movement of the tides welds them into a ball. It was mostly copper but sometimes there'd be a nugget of gold in the middle. If you found a ball – especially one with a gold heart – then you were made. The main thing was to hide it so that no one else tried to rob you. Children who found a ball used to stay till last in the sewer so that no one would see them. Sometimes they stayed too long and got caught by the tide and drowned. Just when they had struck it rich.'

She held his arm tight. The gold pieces had been taken from the river and the mist was thickening, like curls of damp grey hair. Again there was a crack of breaking wood behind them; Blackstone took no notice because he was stalking the muddy streets and crawling the sewers again.

She asked: 'But what happened, Blackie? How did you grow up this way? How did you get to Bow Street?'

She seemed to be guiding him through the woods; but he was only vaguely aware of it.

He told her: 'I teamed up with a gang of boys. After a while, as the law had caught up with its senior members, one by one, I became their leader – their arch-cove. We used to rob the drunks around Piccadilly, and the blades when they took girls into Hyde Park. When I was a boy Hyde Park was worse than the Dials. And it's not much better now.' He stopped. 'We'd better be getting back to the horses.' The afternoon was now meant for tea and toast and fires. They turned and walked back along the scuffed trail they had left in the wet leaves.

'Then what happened? Why aren't you a criminal now?'

'A lot of people think I still am.'

'What happened, Blackie?' She was hurrying him along as if there were going to be a storm.

'I was lucky. I was pinched stealing one day by an old man who took pity on me. He hadn't got any children of his own.

G 97

He didn't take me into his home or anything like that. But he made me report to him every few days. He taught me to read and write and speak a bit better than I did. I was still thieving although he didn't know it. A pretty dangerous occupation it was too – a boy of fourteen was hanged for stealing linen when I was pinching gold watches. When I was eighteen I was still robbing. In fact I burgled a couple of houses at about that time. Old bastards who were getting rich cramming kids into lodging houses. Then my old gentleman died and left me £50 on the condition that I signed on at Bow Street. He knew the magistrate there at the time. It seemed a good idea anyway. Less chance of getting topped or transported for life. So I went on the foot patrols. Then I got promoted to the Runners. I also went on reading as much as I could and trying to speak a little better than my colleagues. And here I am with you in the woods having just been dismissed as Royal nursemaid. Nothing heroic, you see. Nothing noble. Everything I've done has been done in the interests of Edmund Blackstone who never robbed the rich to give to the poor in his life. I was lucky I was only caught once, I was lucky that it was a kind old man who caught me. Everything was luck. But life is luck – and knowing what to do with it.'

'I wish,' she said, 'I knew who your father was.'

'Why?'

'So that I could have some clues about you.'

'You've got enough, surely.'

'No, there's more to you than just a tough upbringing. You like cricket. Perhaps he was a cricketer.'

'A swordsman at any rate,' Blackstone said.

'You're interested in this new railway. Perhaps he was an engineer. But I think he was probably George IV when he was a young man.'

'God forbid.'

'You do the King an injustice. He might be corrupt but he's artistic and sensitive. And you're very sensitive.'

She leaned against him and pulled his head down to kiss him. But managed to push him to one side as the shot rang out.

The ball smacked into an old tree trunk on a level with his head, lodging deep in the rotting wood. One barrel gone. But if he were a professional assassin – if he were Challoner – he would have one more barrel on the pistol he had fired, two more guns ready. Another five to go. Blackie pulled Jane Hatherley on to the ground.

'You arranged this, didn't you?'

'No,' she said. 'No, Blackie. I swear. . . . '

'You bitch.' He put his hand over her mouth and listened. A footstep beyond a thicket of bracken and brambles crunching on dead leaves.

He drew one of the flintlock holster pistols converted to percussion he had stuck in his belt. Simple and accurate, but only one barrel. But he had presumed he was only going riding with a lady. You're getting careless, Blackstone.

Another blurred footstep. The crack of a twig. A blackbird flapping away squawking a warning. A hundred yards away the river slurred past with the mist settling a foot high across it.

Blackstone crawled behind the wounded tree trunk pulling the girl with him. 'You stay here,' he whispered. 'I'm going round the back of him.'

'He'll kill you.'

'So? That's what you wanted, wasn't it?'

'No, Blackie,' she said. 'No.'

But he was gone.

Behind the bracken he saw a movement. Heard the sterile click of a pistol misfiring. A bad conversion, a dud cap.

Blackstone aimed at the movement and fired. The ball carved a furrow through the thicket. But there was no cry of pain.

He wondered how much trouble the pistol was giving the assassin. But he would have another gun, two perhaps.

He stuck the Perry conversion back into his belt and brought out its twin. He could have done with the old blunder-buss converted to percussion which a pikeman had given him. One more shot and he was a sitting target while he reloaded. He decided to try and head back to the horses.

The next ball was high, cannoning through the branches

out to the river. Blackstone thought he heard it splash down, but he couldn't be sure. He ran for cover and continued to back towards the towpath, waiting for the next shot.

He looked at his pistol, felt the neat rounded barrel still warm from his body. Just one good sight of the man was all he needed. It was a neat executioner, the Perry conversion.

He ran for an oak tree expecting to hear a shot. Nothing. He crouched among the leaves and acorns, smelling the mud.

But instead of a shot he heard a man's shout. And Jane Hatherley's voice. And scuffling.

He peered round the trunk of the tree. Then ran back towards the two figures swaying together a hundred yards away.

When he was fifty yards away the man broke free and ran to the left, making for a curve in the river where he had probably tethered his horse.

Blackstone stopped and took aim. But the man was zig-zagging his way towards the protection of the mist nestling on the river.

Blackstone stuck his pistol in his belt without firing it. He saw the man mount a horse tethered beside the black hulk of a barge. He ran for Poacher, jumped into the saddle in one movement and gave chase.

He was vaguely aware that Jane Hatherley was running through the woods calling to him.

Horse and rider were phantoms on the towpath leading to the road. Blackstone urged on Poacher but the horse in front was fast. Not as fast as Poacher was when he was fit, but fast enough to keep ahead today.

The horseman ahead was using the whip, his cloak streaming behind him. When he reached the road he turned left and headed towards Kensington.

Blackstone was delayed by a coach. He could hardly see his quarry any more. He asked Poacher for a fraction more speed: the outline became more distinct.

Then very distinct. Blackstone realized that he had stopped

and was aiming a rifle which must have been strapped to his horse.

He ducked. The explosion lit the thickening afternoon. Blackstone felt heat; Poacher whinnied with pain.

Blackstone aimed his pistol and fired back. But the phantom was dissolving into the gloom. The echoes of the shots lost themselves while the afternoon reassembled itself.

Blackstone dismounted and examined Poacher. The ball had grazed the horse's shoulder. There was a pink wound the size of a man's hand on the shoulder. Blackstone stroked his neck and spoke gently into his ear. The horse shivered and pawed the ground. 'Don't worry,' Blackstone said. 'We'll get you good treatment. You'll be fine. You did well and if he hadn't had that rifle we'd have caught him.'

Maybe, he thought. Maybe not. But one thing's certain – we *will* catch him. Because even in the uncertain light the tall heavy figure running through the woods beside the river had unmistakenly been that of Sir Rupert Charlston.

Chapter Twelve

·✤·

WITH Blackstone gone, Lawler felt the responsibility as acutely as a hangover. Blackstone had told him to watch practically everyone in the Palace; in particular he had told him to watch Page. Page, Blackstone had warned him, would be after him.

Which he was. Within a few minutes of their meeting Page suggested that Lawler might know something about the missing miniature. He asked him if they'd ever met before. By which he meant had he ever arrested Lawler. Lawler said they hadn't met.

Page suggested that Blackstone protected him and told him that this was the sort of set-up that Parliamentary committees of inquiry would be looking into. Criminal contacts, informers, corrupt deals in flash taverns. And Lawler wouldn't want to get involved in anything at Parliamentary level, would he? So why didn't he co-operate?

By which Page meant why didn't they try and betray Blackstone together. He was told to go to hell.

Page became vicious and ordered him to turn out his pockets in case they contained anything on his list. They didn't; but Lawler thought Page wouldn't be beyond planting a watch or wallet on him within the next few days.

He had always felt safe with Blackstone backing him. Now Blackstone was in trouble himself.

Also Lawler's sex life was becoming complicated.

The nurse, Mary Singleton, was as greedy for sex as she was for her green and pink sugared biscuits. He did what was required and found she was competent; trained, he suspected, by the butler, because the butler was angry about their friendship.

The lady's-maid Irma had also become enthusiastic. She told him he was the first man she had been able to relax with since she adopted the Swiss pretence. (She came from Camberwell, of theatrical stock, and had briefly earned a living on the stage playing continental maids.) But her enthusiasm was such that she fed him with whatever information she thought he needed irrespective of truth: laudanum, arsenic, strychnine – all were *missing* from the still-room.

But every discovery she made on his behalf seemed to beckon him towards a terrace cottage in Camberwell. The assistant footman and the lady's-maid. And their dairy-faced babies. Lawler bought her sweetmeats, making them an additional item on his fixed payment of £20, and asked her to confine herself to facts.

Amy Hucklestone, though, defeated him. He had always been able to assess people and negotiate with them from a position of strength. But with Amy Hucklestone there didn't seem to be anything to assess: just a wilderness of honesty without a single hold.

Lawler thought he might be in love with her.

Although he wasn't sure whether it was Lawler the footman or Lawler the chancer who felt that way.

He communicated most of this to Blackstone when they met in the evening at the new five-arched stone bridge built by George Rennie across the Serpentine.

Lawler made his point first. He said: 'I think you should pay me more money. I've got a lot more responsibility now.'

'You're being paid too much as it is.'

Lawler gazed into the evil-smelling water across which, when frozen, a Mr Hunt had attempted to drive a coach and four for a bet last year. Lawler remembered this without pleasure because he had taken several bets that Mr Hunt would make it, which he had.

He said: 'Things aren't the same any more, are they, Mr Blackstone?'

'What do you mean?' Blackstone asked.

'You can't protect me any more. Come to think of it, can you pay me any more?'

'I'll pay you,' Blackstone said. 'And I'll protect you.'

Lawler continued to stare unhappily into the water which accepted sewage from many parts of London. 'I don't see how you can protect me like you used to. I'm not saying I want protection. I can look after myself. But when I'm on a job like this I need some backing. . . . '

Blackstone said: 'I'm still a Bow Street Runner, Lawler.' He took the baton out of his pocket. 'No one will attack us here while I'm carrying this.'

Figures flitted around them: Lawler wasn't entirely convinced. But he thought he was closer to friendship with Blackstone than ever before. 'I know what it must feel like. . . . '

'How the hell can you know?'

'You know . . . having this thing hanging over you.'

Blackstone said: 'When I need your sympathy I'll let you know. At the moment I'm still a Runner. And you'll go on doing what I tell you. Otherwise I'll have you in a cell as quick as that.' He snapped his fingers. 'Now I believe some sort of attempt is going to be made on the Princess. I didn't before but I do now. I want every piece of information you can lay your hands on. Above stairs, below stairs. Because there must be someone working inside the Palace.'

'I understand,' Lawler said, thinking that in the present circumstances it would be very easy to tell Blackstone to jump in the Serpentine.

Lawler considered telling Blackstone about the money he was losing from his customers. He didn't bother. If only Blackstone could try and be a bit more reasonable. It wasn't as if he'd always been on the side of the law. It wasn't as if he would be much longer. . . .

Lawler asked: 'What am I supposed to do about Page?'

'Nothing,' Blackstone said.

'That's all very well. . . . '

'If he tries to pin anything on you tell him I'll kill him.'

'And would you?'

The evening light had gone but the stars were as thick as snowflakes. Blackstone turned to him so that all Lawler could see was the shadow of his face and the hard light of the moon and the stars in his eyes. 'Of course I would.'

'What, just because he planted some evidence on me?'

'Just that,' Blackstone said.

Lawler pondered on this while the stars in the deep night glimmered about an eternity of double-dealing.

'I'll tell him that,' Lawler said.

'You do,' said Blackstone.

Chapter Thirteen

••✥••

BLACKSTONE selected two Manton holster pistols, heavy and commanding with octagonal casing round the barrel, and a screw-barrel pocket pistol by John Barton. Into one of his riding boots he slipped an 18-inch-long French Naval dirk which he had taken from a French spy operating from a house in Pimlico five years ago. It was thin and vicious with blue and gold patterns at the base of the blade and a leather sheath which Blackstone didn't bother with. Then he went to see how Poacher was; the wound looked healthy and the horse seemed happy. He took another horse, a grey, which he had borrowed, and slid the pistols in beside the saddle. Then he went looking for three men.

But first he saw Birnie, before the magistrate went into Court. Birnie looked cold and worried and angry. Blackstone told him about Challoner and Birnie said he had heard about Blackstone's suspicions. But Page was in charge now; and Conroy had decided against putting a foot patrol into the area because it would attract attention. 'But,' Birnie told him, 'we are looking for Challoner.'

'You won't find him,' Blackstone said.

Birnie looked at Blackstone speculatively, one finger rubbing a patch of grey stubble on his chin that the razor had missed. 'I don't want *you* looking for him,' he said. 'You're suspended. Understand?'

Blackstone looked at him and thought that maybe he was too old for the job. The magisterial duties, the Runners, the patrols, the accelerating struggle with Peel, who was still under forty. His face was straight from the Scottish moors today – when the heather has faded and the gorse is dead.

'Understand, Blackstone?'

'Yes, sir. I understand.'

He went across the road to the Brown Bear for a drink before going about his business. George Ruthven was there drinking with Townsend.

'So,' Ruthven said, sipping his brandy, 'you decide it's Challoner. Why? Because a lot of flash gentry down at Sol's Arms tell you it's Challoner. Every one of them knows that you've got a private fight with Challoner. Don't you think it's possible, Blackie, that they're enjoying themselves at your expense? God knows, you've arrested enough of them in your time. And stopped them pulling enough jobs. You don't imagine they like you, do you?'

Blackstone drank some ale and stared across the street at their headquarters. 'It was Challoner all right,' he said.

'For God's sake, what proof have you?'

'My intuition,' Blackstone told him.

'His intuition! Isn't that wonderful?' Ruthven appealed to Townsend, the great Townsend.

Townsend, associate of Royalty and aristocracy, shrugged.

Blackstone asked: 'Do you know Challoner, Townsend?'

Townsend said: 'I never met him. I have the greatest respect for him, though.'

Blackstone remembered the days when he regarded Townsend as the greatest policeman in the world. As he probably had been. Blackstone understood Townsend. He had been great: he was old: he was entitled to his lordly airs.

Townsend said: 'Wasn't he the villain who escaped from Cato Street?'

Blackstone said: 'Yes, and I was the Runner who lost him.'

'That was your first job as a Runner, wasn't it? I can't think of a more worthy opponent to be beaten by.'

Was that fair? Beaten? He had been bleeding from the wound in the hip. Still, Challoner had been the only man to get completely away. And it had been Blackstone's first job as a fully-paid Bow Street Runner.

Blackstone wondered, as he had wondered many times before, about Challoner's parentage. There was no evidence, just a presentiment, like the knowledge that you are being watched.

He went first to the Admiralty Sessions where a man called Thomas Young stood accused of slave trading.

Young, the Master of a brig called the *Malta*, had been trading for gum and ivory on the West Coast of Africa. Until the Africans kept their side of the bargain Young had taken four hostages – as was the custom, the court was told.

Blackstone listened with interest to the manner in which witnesses referred to the Africans, as if they were almost human.

He smelled the compost depths of the jungle. He smelled corruption; he smelled the sea.

The hostages were four girls called Nourah, Pikinini, Jumbo Jack and Quarbel. Well-built girls, according to some of Young's crew who alleged that they had been stripped for inspection.

The crew claimed that Young had broken his word with the African traders and sold the girls to a Spanish slave ship anchored nearby. Young had asked sixty dollars per girl but had settled for twenty-eight.

But there was a strong suspicion of mutiny on board the *Malta*. And the court accepted Young's version that the crew had made up the story to anticipate any proceedings taken against them.

Young was acquitted.

The sailors left with various lawyers employed in case they were arrested and charged with mutiny. Among the small-time lawyers was Benjamin Darnley, just as the perch of lawyers in Sol's Arms had said he would be.

He was a small moist man, full of court manners and rhetoric; but he had no conviction or sustained argument behind his utterances; his words dribbled away and he hammered home points with a mallet of wet cardboard. If you were charged with burglary, Blackstone thought, Darnley was the defending lawyer to get you convicted of murder.

Blackstone stopped him beside a waiting cab.

'Good morning, Mr Darnley,' he said.

Darnley smiled, hoping for another brief, as his sailors rolled away leaving him with salty handshakes and no payments. 'Good morning,' he said, 'is there anything I can do for you?'

Blackstone nodded pleasantly. 'There is. I want to know who paid you to write that complaint and threatening letter to Birnie.'

'You're Blackstone.'

Blackstone nodded, showing the lawyer his baton. Darnley was very pink and speckled, as if he roasted his face over a tavern fire every evening. He tried to disguise the fear with indignation.

He said: 'Look here, Blackstone, you keep away from me. You're in enough trouble as it is.' He sensed implacable forces and tried to reason with Blackstone. 'It's in your own interests, you know. Interfering with the course of justice won't help you . . .' His words died as if he were used to being cut short by judge and magistrate.

'Justice?' Blackstone tasted the word. 'What justice?'

'I mean to see that these men you've beaten get justice.'

Blackstone grinned. 'Have you seen these men?'

'Of course I've seen them.'

'And what would they know about justice, Mr Darnley? What would you for that matter?'

'Look here, Blackstone,' Darnley said. 'I've got to be getting along. You leave me alone and I'll forget you ever approached me.'

Blackstone pointed to the cab. 'Get in,' he said.

'I will not.'

Blackstone jabbed him in the ribs with his pocket pistol. 'Get in, Darnley.'

Darnley was trembling violently. 'You can't do this, Blackstone. You mustn't . . .'

Blackstone shoved him with the barrel of the pistol and he half fell into the cab. Blackstone sat beside him. The cabby, an accomplice of old, whipped up the horses and they headed down the Strand.

Blackstone stroked the gun, looking thoughtfully at the lawyer. He wore a black top-coat made for a bigger man and a tall black hat with a pouting brim. He struck the raised hood with his cane but the driver took no notice.

Blackstone said: 'If I shot you he wouldn't take any notice.'

'This will finish you,' Darnley said. 'Absolutely finish you . . .'

'You're going to finish me anyway, aren't you, Darnley? So what does it matter to me? Now tell me who's behind all this. I haven't got much time.'

'I can't disclose the name of a client. It's against legal etiquette.'

Blackstone toyed with the hammer of the stubby gun.

Darnley said: 'You wouldn't.'

'I would,' Blackstone said.

Darnley's hand strayed hesitantly towards his coat pocket. Blackstone leaned across and relieved him of a three-barrelled pistol with an ornate silver lock. Darnley looked almost pleased, as if he didn't know how to use it anyway.

The cab lunged right towards Covent Garden.

Blackstone gave him another prod. 'So, Darnley, what have you got to say?'

'Nothing,' Darnley said, sticking out his baby lower lip.

'In that case I shall kill you when I've counted to ten.' He began to count, holding the pistol loosely with his right hand and taking snuff from his tiny gold box.

Darnley gave it to six. 'I'll see you in court for this,' he warned first.

'I hope you're prosecuting,' Blackstone told him. He put the snuff box away. 'Now first let me tell you what I know, Darnley. I know that you were employed by a man called Henry Challoner to fake this complaint against me.'

Darnley looked surprised. 'I thought that was what you wanted to know.'

'I want to know more than that. I want to know who was behind Challoner. Henry Challoner is a hired assassin.' He noticed the alarm. 'Didn't you know that? Not a man to doublecross, Darnley. Not the sort of man who would take it too kindly if he heard that you had blabbed.'

'But I haven't.'

'But he doesn't know that.' He rested the pistol on his knee. 'Don't worry. I won't tell him. If you find out a few things for me. . . .'

'I don't know anything more.' He took off his hat, revealing a ring of sweat under his soft hair.

'Now listen to me. Challoner didn't employ you for his own purposes. Indirectly, maybe, because he thought I might recognize him. Because we're old enemies. But that's not the point. Challoner was working on something at Kensington Palace. I want to know who was paying him.'

'But I don't know, Blackstone.' Darnley rubbed at the band of sweat with a soiled white handkerchief. 'So help me, I don't know.'

Blackstone decided he was telling the truth.

The cab, as instructed, turned and headed towards the City, going in circles until Blackstone gave the order to stop.

'Tell me,' Blackstone asked, 'why do you think Challoner wanted me out of the way? What did he say?'

'I don't know. He didn't give a reason. And I didn't ask. . . .'

'Because he was paying you well?'

'He paid me quite well, yes.'

'Where can I find him?'

'He came to my office in Wapping. He didn't give an address.'

'And that was sufficient for you to fake evidence?'

'It wasn't faked. You did beat the groom. There's too much of that sort of thing . . .' His voice died on him as was its custom.

'The evidence of the other *complainants* was faked.'

'I didn't know that. I merely took statements from them.'

Blackstone put his gun away. 'I don't think, Mr Darnley, that you quite understand what you're getting involved in. Has it occurred to you that this is something much more sinister than a campaign against me?'

Darnley said it hadn't; but his bothered face looked as if he could be convinced.

Blackstone told him about the rumours of a plot involving Princess Alexandrina Victoria. 'The future Queen of England, Darnley. Think about that. Didn't you wonder what I was doing at the Palace – a Bow Street Runner?'

'I thought you were investigating the theft of a miniature.'

'Did you indeed? Then why was I at the Palace before the miniature was missed?'

'I didn't know you were.' Implications were sinking into Darnley like indictments.

'Supposing that something did happen to Her Royal Highness. Who was the man who got rid of Edmund Blackstone, the Bow Street Runner who was on to something? Why, Benjamin Darnley, advocate, of Wapping. You might become a figure in history yet, Darnley. The lawyer who sold the heir to the throne's life for a few pounds. And don't think Challoner will come to your rescue. I'm sure you haven't got his signature on anything, have you?'

The pink left Darnley's face. 'What are we to do?' he whispered. 'What are we to do?'

'You can help me find Challoner.'

'How can I do that?'

'Challoner will be in touch with you. If I know him he will want that complaint published in the *Morning Herald* whether I'm thrown out of the force or not. When he does, let me know.'

'But how?'

'You'll think of a way,' Blackstone said; because it was all a bit remote anyway, and Darnley didn't know as much as he had hoped he would.

They were approaching the courts again. Blackstone told

the driver to stop. 'Out you get,' he said to Darnley in a kindly voice. 'Go and find yourself a good lawyer – you may need one.'

He told the driver to take him to the Duke of Cumberland's apartments at St James's Palace.

As they pulled up outside the Palace this crisp afternoon a phaeton pulled out. Seated in it was a plump figure with a white face clownishly rouged. A man engaged upon a lifelong courtship with himself. Before he was seventeen he was said by Charles James Fox to be 'rather too fond of women and and wine'. The aesthete who drugged his sensibilities with indulgence. The linguist with the dirty tongue. The guest who arrived in Dublin too drunk to talk. The King of England.

Beside the King sat Lady Conyngham, the current favourite.

Blackstone looked at him speculatively. Was any of this worth it? For such a Monarchy? For a system that could allow a corrupt fat fool to stay on the throne? He thought about the girl at Kensington Palace who might change all that and knew that it was worth it.

The phaeton moved off in the thin sunlight, but no one bothered to wave.

He showed his baton to the Guard and entered the courtyard of the Palace. The Duke of Cumberland had his apartments to the right. Blackstone went up the stairs to the first floor and knocked at the door.

The lair of the man at the heart of the rumours. The one protagonist he hadn't met. Ernest August, Duke of Cumberland and Teviotdale, Earl of Armagh; Governor of Chester and Chancellor of Trinity College, Dublin; fifth son of George III; fearless soldier and leader of the Orangemen; murderer, lecher, and scar-faced, one-eyed bigot according to some; not content with murdering his own valet he had married a twice-widowed German princess rumoured to have murdered her previous two husbands.

A manservant answered the door. A remote-looking man

beautifully dressed, with a wine-coloured cravat at his neck. The successor to the valet Sellis who had been found with his throat cut sixteen years before? A brave or very well-paid man to take the job.

'The Duke of Cumberland,' Blackstone said. 'Is he in?'

The valet, if that's what he was, said: 'Mr Blackstone?'

Blackstone said that was his name.

'We've been expecting you, sir.'

Why? Blackstone wondered.

'Then perhaps I could come in,' he said.

'Certainly, sir. But I'm afraid His Royal Highness is not present.'

Blackstone stepped into a thick-carpeted hallway surveyed by a gallery of noble ancestors immobilized in oils.

'Where is he?'

'In Hanover, sir.'

'What the hell's he doing over there?'

The manservant grinned suddenly and swallowed the genteel lozenge stuck in his throat. 'Keeping out of your way, I shouldn't be surprised.'

Blackstone laughed, thinking that he could do with a bit of flattery. 'Tell me,' he said, 'why were you expecting me?'

The manservant, middle-aged with greying hair combed forward over his temples, said that information had reached the Household that a Bow Street Runner had been sent to Kensington Palace to guard the Princess.

'Is that why Cumberland went to Germany?'

'No. It was something to do with the Hanoverian Hussars. He won't be back for a week.'

'A bit of a coincidence, isn't it?'

'I don't think so. It's been on his diary for months.'

Nevertheless, Blackstone thought, if anything was going to happen to the Princess it was in Cumberland's interests to be out of the way.

He said: 'So you're all on your own here?'

'More or less. One or two other servants have been left behind.'

'And you've taken the opportunity to wear some of your master's clothes, I see.'

The manservant's hand went straight to the cravat. 'Your reputation is well founded, Mr Blackstone. I hope you're not going to arrest me for it.'

Blackstone shook his head. 'But don't let him find out when he returns. Otherwise . . .' With his finger Blackstone cut his own throat from ear to ear.

The manservant grinned. 'I may be a bit old in the tooth but I'm a match for the Duke.'

'Is he as bad as he's painted?'

'He's all right,' the manservant said. 'If you're not a Catholic.'

'I hope you're a good Protestant,' Blackstone said.

'I'm a good anything if the pay's right,' the manservant told him. 'By the way,' he added, 'you just missed someone else from Kensington Palace. Lady Jane Hatherley was over here looking for His Royal Highness.'

The third man Blackstone went looking for was Sir Rupert Charlston. But when he found him he was dead.

Chapter Fourteen

⸙

CHARLSTON had been put to the sword in a duel on Putney Heath that morning.

Blackstone had been on the Heath at dawn on previous occasions acting on one of the many tips of forthcoming duels the Bow Street Runners received. He could imagine the scene.

The carriages waiting on the road with the first birds singing as the sun spread lemon-coloured light on a highwayman's skyline of trees and thickets; the light brightening, setting fire to the clouds on such an autumn morning. Frost crusting the ground, tissues of ice on the puddles, a roaming wind.

In the carriages there might be eight or so gentlemen. Friends, seconds, surgeons. The surgeons with their instruments, two other men with the weapons. If they were guns, and the duellists had some class, they might be by Joseph Manton. Beautiful pistols, half-stocked with a horn fore-end; the browned barrels ribbed underneath. Frizzen spring fitted with a cam engaging a roller. A thick heavy barrel ten inches long, .5-inch bore. That year Manton had gone bankrupt. People didn't want beautiful guns any more: just instruments with which to kill each other. Perhaps they were right. Why inscribe murder with beauty? Not that any of this changed Blackstone's love of aristocratic firearms – the power and the beauty fusing in your hand.

He imagined the men alighting from the carriages with two look-outs posted behind the thicket hiding the duellists. The flames in the sky dying, a handful of disturbed birds circling.

They took the agreed number of steps to death, injury or continuing life, turned and fired. The explosions sealing the dawn, the smell of gunpowder as crisp as the frost.

If one died then his opponent might be charged with manslaughter, and acquitted after token punishment – the burning of the hand. Murder dressed up and applauded.

But Charlston's death had been more sinister than the conventional pantomime of death. Blackstone suspected that Charlston had been murdered by a professional killer.

The duel had been arranged after a man of about thirty called Wilkinson had arrived in town from 'somewhere in the West Country'. He found Charlston drinking in a tavern not far from Kensington Palace and accused him of failing to pay his debts.

Blackstone saw the conceited, heavy-muscled Charlston advancing towards his death like a lion ponderous with easily-killed meat, charging towards a concealed trap. He was reputed to be one of the best swordsmen in London. But only in his class, in his noble circles. There were other circles where men killed to live, where some made it their living. Not for these men any instinct of chivalry taught on the playing-fields of Eton; for them chivalry was a weakness to be exploited. (Not that Charlston was chivalrous, but he would have learned chivalrous manners.) Also the professional killers had a few tricks of their own; an accomplice to create a diversion, a doctored weapon.

Charlston had chosen swords for his suicide, boasting that he was a match for anyone in London. But he was no match for the quiet, intense man, with hair so black that it had blue lights in it, from the West. Charlston was almost middle-aged but didn't know it, and his appetites had slowed him down.

The duel didn't last long. No one seemed too sure how Wilkinson won so quickly. Suddenly Charlston was without his sword, clawing at his eyes according to some accounts; then kneeling. Wilkinson's sword plunged straight through the heart and emerged through Charlston's back.

Then Wilkinson was gone on his big fast horse, cloak streaming behind him. No regrets, no condolences. His job was done and he left in the manner of a busy man who has another job to finish before his day's work is over.

Blackstone imagined Charlston's big body falling heavily. But it was difficult to feel pity for the man who had recently tried to shoot you.

Sitting in his rooms in Paddington, Blackstone considered the murder and other puzzling aspects of the assignment from which he had been dismissed. And he looked around and enjoyed his possessions. He thought he had good taste, he wasn't absolutely sure. The guns on the walls were good: that he did know.

He wasn't so sure of some of his other exhibits. The water-colour by A. V. Copley Fielding given to him after he had guarded an art exhibition in Duke Street, St James's. And on the mantelpiece the Wedgwood water jug with its Neptune figure in black basaltes. He hoped they displayed good taste; but he didn't know because it wasn't something you could acquire.

He poured himself some whisky into an old glass cut by Johnson, one of a set given to him after he had saved some stolen plate from the melters. He lit a lamp and watched the light fractured and scattered around the room by the crystals of the chandelier.

So, he thought, we have a murder. And we have a theft. We have a long and suspicious cast and we have a lot of motives.

But motives for what? The outstanding aspect of the job was that the crime which he had originally been engaged to stop hadn't been committed.

And shortly, if nothing developed, he wouldn't be a Bow Street Runner any longer. He stared at his collectors' pieces, all obtained more or less honestly. If he were sacked he would have to acquire them the old way – and further additions would soon be reported missing in the 'Hue and Cry'.

For the first time that he could remember since childhood Blackstone felt frightened. The sort of fear that presents itself in waking moments during the night and is dispelled by the light. But it was only eight o'clock in the evening.

PART TWO

PART TWO

Chapter One

⸺⸻⸺❖⸻⸺

PRINCESS Alexandrina Victoria was kidnapped at 3.34pm on a warm day inserted into late autumn as she walked in Kensington Gardens with her mother, the Duchess of Kent, and the ubiquitous Fräulein Lehzen.

The kidnappers were lucky because this, the second outing since the Princess's indisposition, had been in doubt. The previous day she had walked only around the Palace grounds. And Fräulein Lehzen had recommended once again confining the outing. But the Duchess thought the longer walk in the unexpected sunshine would do her good; and Sir John Conroy had urged her to let her daughter be seen to discount any rumours that she had been poisoned.

The kidnappers were also lucky that an outbreak of gastric influenza had decimated the staff of Kensington Palace and the only guard accompanying the Princess and the two women that day was the Bow Street Runner Page walking at a discreet seventy-five yards behind them.

It happened with speed and precision.

Two men apparently strolling out of an exit suddenly turned and grabbed the Princess. The Duchess and Fräulein Lehzen screamed and tried to attack the two men. But their blows were moth-wings.

The bigger of the two carried the kicking Princess while the slighter ran behind to repel any rescuers. Both were masked. According to witnesses the second man waved a gun; but the other seemed to be in charge, although no one could say why they presumed that. Something about his manner. And he ran with a slight limp.

Page raced after the kidnappers. But just as he reached the road he fell. Fräulein Lehzen, in one of her few lucid moments between hysterics, said he didn't seem to be in very good condition.

The door of the carriage was open. A black shabby-looking carriage incongruously pulled by two lithe horses with sprinters' muscles.

At the first flick of the driver's whip the horses were off, heading west. The two screaming women reached Page as he staggered to his feet. The three of them stood watching the carriage disappear, the horses' hooves sounding brisk but slightly muffled by the drying mud. The two women were quiet for a few moments, hands praying. Then they began to scream again, voices hoarse with disbelief and terror. Page took a few steps forward, then stopped, hands flickering from pocket to pocket of his torn clothes.

Malt said: 'God, what have we done?'

Princess Alexandrina Victoria sat between them on the soft expensive leather seat, Malt's hand round her mouth.

Challoner said: 'Be quiet.'

'If you feel like that about me I don't know why you asked me to do the job.'

The Princess bit Malt's finger. He yelped. He sucked his finger, allowing her to speak.

She said: 'You'd better take me back immediately or you'll both be executed.'

Malt said: 'I don't like it. I don't like it at all.'

Challoner looked out of the window and realized that Kensington was a long way behind them. He almost smiled. 'You're quite frightened of the little girl, aren't you?'

The Princess, who wore the last straw hat of the season for this surprisingly warm day, a navy blue coat and a light blue dress with a broad frill of white cambric around the neck, waited to see how Malt felt about her.

Malt said: 'You don't seem to realize how serious this is.' Paradoxically, fear had made him bold with Challoner. 'This little bitch is the future Queen of England.'

The Princess nodded. 'They don't seem to think I know it. But it's so obvious. The way they treat me, the things they teach me.'

'You don't seem to be very frightened,' Challoner said.

'I'm frightened all right,' she told him. 'But I mustn't show my feelings.' She sat back in the seat. 'Where are you taking me? And why are you doing this?'

'You needn't worry,' Challoner said. 'No harm will come to you.' His voice sounded almost kindly.

'Why have you both covered your faces?'

Malt said: 'So you can't ever say you recognize us.'

There was only the occasional farmhouse and cottage outside now. The grass in the fields was losing its health and in the trees the crows' nests which had been hidden by the leaves were visible.

Challoner put his hand on her arm, but she recoiled.

Malt said: 'When do we change carriages?'

'Soon,' Challoner told him. 'About half a mile before we go through the turnpike.'

The Princess asked: 'Are you going to kill me?'

Challoner shook his head.

'Then why *have* you taken me prisoner?' Her voice quavered for the first time.

'It's a long and complicated story,' Challoner said.

'Is it to do with Uncle Ernest?'

'You needn't worry who it's to do with. Just tell yourself that it's to do with grown-ups. That some of them want you out of the way for a while.'

She had begun to tremble. 'Have you ever killed any-one?'

Challoner was silent.

Malt said: 'He's killed more than you've had hot dinners.'

Challoner stared at him menacingly.

'Well you have, haven't you . . .?'

'If you mention my name,' Challoner interrupted, 'I'll kill you.'

The Princess said: 'I want to cry but I know I mustn't.'

'Cry as much as you like,' Malt said. And then: 'I never knew it was going to be like this.'

'Like what?' Challoner asked.

'I don't know. I didn't realize how serious it was going to be. You know, having her in the carriage with us.'

'You knew,' Challoner said.

'We could be hanged for this.'

'Hanged?' Challoner laughed. You'd be hanged, drawn and quartered if you were caught. And you'd have the whole country howling for your blood. Don't forget that.' He told the Princess: 'You see, that's why we have to keep our faces covered. And I'm afraid we still have to blindfold you for a while so that you don't see where you are.'

'Mama will be in a terrible state,' she said.

'Not just mama,' Challoner observed.

They turned down a lane and stopped outside a whitewashed farmhouse with Tudor beams. Outside stood a shining blue and maroon carriage with staid horses between the shafts. A fine new carriage fit for a queen.

The Princess was locked in a downstairs room with the farmer while they pushed the black carriage into a barn. They covered it with hay so that when they had finished it looked like a stack.

All the time they worked Malt talked, his handsome uncertain face frowning with worry. 'She's such a clever little bitch,' he said. 'She'll finish us. She'll recognize us. I wish to Christ I'd never got involved. I must have been mad – the future Queen of England.' He spoke to himself because Challoner acted as if he weren't there. 'I'll never be able to show my face in London again. I'll be on the run for the rest of my life.'

Challoner said: 'You take one horse, I'll take the other.'

They led the two horses to a stable behind a copse where they fed them and covered them with blankets.

Malt asked: 'Mr Challoner, are you sure we'd be hung, drawn and quartered?'

'Quite sure, Malt. And you know what that means. They cut you down before you're dead. Then they cut your parts off and pull your bowels out. You're then quartered and taken from Newgate. As a last gesture they cut your head off and rip out your stomach and heart. Just to make sure that you won't give any more trouble.'

Malt began to tremble. 'Christ,' he said, 'I feel sick. I don't know why . . .'

'You did it,' Challoner interrupted, 'because of the money. £25 when you undertook the job. Another £75 when it's finished. That's why you took the job, Malt. For the same reason as me.'

'I didn't know it was going to be like this.'

'What the hell did you think it was going to be like?'

'I didn't realize the whole country would be looking for us.' He paused as they closed the doors of the stable. 'The military will be after us most likely.'

'Most likely,' Challoner agreed.

Malt leaned on the door considering this. 'Mr Challoner . . .'

'Yes, Malt?'

'Have you ever thought about killing her so she can't talk?'

Challoner said: 'Those aren't our orders.'

'Just what are our orders?'

'They needn't concern you. Now get going, Malt. We've got about ten minutes. They don't know which road we took but they'll be checking every turnpike.'

Malt tied the cloth back round his face. 'What more do you want from me, Mr Challoner?'

'Not a great deal,' Challoner said. 'Why?'

'If I could get out now . . . I mean you can manage better on your own. I wouldn't even ask for the rest of the money. £25 is a handsome sum of money. And I'll never blab, Mr Challoner. That I'd never do.'

Challoner retied the black cloth around his face. He said: 'You've done well, Malt.'

Malt smiled uncertainly.

'You really want to pull out now?'

'I'd like to, Mr Challoner.'

'Very well, Malt.'

Casually, Challoner put his hand into his overcoat pocket as if he were getting out a handkerchief. Instead he took out a pocket pistol bearing the name Parker and the words 'Maker to His Majesty, London'.

'No,' Malt said. 'No, Mr Challoner.' He backed away, hand reaching for his own pistol.

Challoner said: 'You did a good job, Malt.'

He shot him through the heart. Then put another ball through his head, destroying his handsome features. Afterwards he went through Malt's pockets removing anything identifiable. He didn't take the money: he didn't plunder bodies.

He gave the farmer who had been watching the Princess another £50 in sovereigns and half-sovereigns and told him to hide the body and then bury it.

The Princess was sitting on the edge of a bed, the blindfold still around her eyes. A brave little girl, Challoner thought. He spoke as gently as he was able. 'We're going for another ride now. Don't be frightened. I know that's impossible but I want you to know that no one's going to hurt you. You'll have to keep the blindfold on for a little longer. When we get to our next destination you can take it off.'

'Why are you doing this to me?'

'It's not for me to say.'

'Where's the other man?'

'He's not coming any farther with us.'

'I heard a shot just now . . .'

'A farmer killing crows.'

'I'm glad he's not coming with us. I trust you more.'

'Why?' Challoner asked.

'I don't know. Something about you.'

It was, Challoner reflected, the first time that anyone had placed trust in him for many years. It made him uneasy.

'Now,' he told her, 'I'm going to have to put something round your mouth in case you call out as we pass the turnpike. There may be other carriages there.'

'I won't call out.'

'I'm afraid I don't believe you. You've got too much spirit.'

He tied a bandage round her mouth and sank back into a corner of the seat. The next stage was up to the driver, a reliable footpad who had worked with Challoner before. All he had to do was to remind the pikeman that he hadn't seen them – in case the pursuers found out about the new coach – and pay the toll. In this case £50. A lot of beautiful gold was changing hands, Challoner reflected. But he supposed heirs to the throne came expensive.

The wheels of the carriage ground on gravel. The drive led up to a red-brick mansion with many windows and chimneys and a terrace with tall stone plant pots posted like sentries. It was surrounded by a high beech hedge and, beyond that, a ring of rich grassland, then forest. The gardens had been laid out with too much geometric care: this seemed to prevent it from being a stately home.

It was dusk and the country air smelled of mist and frost. No owls hooted; but you could imagine them.

Challoner took her to a small room on the first floor. A coal fire burned and there was some supper on the table. In the corner stood a single bed. Beside it some picture books.

He took the blindfold off, still keeping his mask on. 'There,' he said.

She looked around, rubbing her eyes. He thought she was a pretty little girl.

She examined the books and told him: 'These are for five-year-olds. I'm seven.'

Challoner said: 'I'll see if I can find something else. A house-keeper will be here shortly to look after you.'

'I don't want anyone.'

'What – and have you climbing down the drainpipe?' He smiled behind the mask, hoping his eyes smiled too.

'I'm tired of having people sleep with me anyway. Mama always sleeps on a bed beside me.' Her voice broke a little and she turned away.

There was a knock on the door and a plump woman with grey hair combed into a bun came in. It was a country face with some hard London lines in it. She looked nervous though. Challoner thought: Another £50.

He left them together and went to the room where he was to sleep. Later he thought he heard her crying but he couldn't be sure.

Before sleep Challoner thought about Blackstone. Almost his double, except for the accidents of maturing. A man to respect: a man to kill: otherwise one day he would kill you. Sometimes it seemed as if there were just the two of them pitted against each other. Born in different homes but perhaps from a single source. It was possible in the brick, seed-blown thickets of Holborn. He wondered about it and knew that Blackstone did the same. They eyed each other across the boundaries drawn by accident and saw how it might have been. Challoner acknowledged his jealousy; then slept.

Chapter Two

BLACKSTONE spoke to Page in the corridor of No. 4 Bow Street where Page was awaiting a summons from Birnie. Birnie also had to meet the Prime Minister, Lord Liverpool, the Duke of Wellington possibly, Peel certainly.

Page was resentful and scared. He described the black carriage to Blackstone and what he could remember of the two men. 'One had a slight limp,' he said.

'Challoner,' Blackstone said.

'Maybe,' Page said. He paused. 'I didn't stand a chance, Blackstone. Not a chance. It would have been just the same if you had been there. What do you think they'll do, Blackie?'

'Shoot you,' Blackstone said.

He tried to slot himself into Challoner's mind. It wasn't difficult. Where would I go?

He said: 'I suppose they've got troops and horse patrols out?'

Page nodded. 'But they only know they're looking for this black carriage. And the horses, of course – I described those quite accurately. One chestnut with a blaze on its head, the other jet black.'

'I would change those,' Blackstone said.

'What do you mean, *you* would change them?'

'If I were Challoner.'

He thought: And I'd also change the carriage. He snapped his fingers. They were all looking for the wrong carriage. But where would I change it? I would get as many miles as possible between me and Kensington. That's what the fast horses were for. So the crucial points would be whatever turnpikes I had to pass. If there were no reports of the black carriage with those two horses passing the turnpikes then the pursuers would presume their quarry was still inside the toll points. So I'd change horses *and* carriage just this side of the turnpike.

He turned to Page. 'Good luck,' he said. 'You need it.'

He went to the main office and got out maps. The carriage had headed west. Not Windsor. That was the last direction Challoner would take. Blackstone bisected the angle between west and north and noted Oxford. Somewhere in that direction.

He looked at his watch. It was 8am. He went upstairs to Birnie's room, knocked and went in.

Birnie held up his hands. 'Not now, Blackstone. Whatever it is, not now. I have to be in Whitehall in one hour. This could be the end of us.'

'Or the making of us,' Blackstone said.

Birnie looked up from his desk. 'Have you taken leave of your senses?' The skin on his face seemed to have loosened and his grey hair was dishevelled.

'I think I might be able to find them.'

'How?'

Blackstone told him, minimizing the conjecture.

Birnie said: 'I can't face Liverpool – and Peel – with a theory like that. They see it in very simple terms. They entrusted the Princess into the care of the Bow Street Runners and we lost her. Peel will never let up now.'

Blackstone said: 'Look at it this way, sir. The rumours were never taken very seriously. Otherwise more precautions would have been taken. The Army would have been moved in. The fact is that Page and I were only sent to the Palace to keep the Duchess happy. So really the error is in much higher places than Bow Street.' With Peel, he implied. 'With respect, sir, you mustn't see the ministers in a defensive frame of mind. You must create the impression that it's they who are at fault – but the Bow Street Runners might yet be able to save the day.'

Birnie walked over to the dying fire and poked the embers. 'If the ministers accept your theories . . .'

'I suggest they become *your* theories, sir.'

'If the ministers accept the theories they'll order troops into the area. Search every building until they find her.'

'Then they'd lose her. The kidnappers would flee. They might even murder her.'

'If they haven't already done so.'

'If they haven't already done so,' Blackstone agreed. 'Although I don't think they have. Not if they want ransom.'

'Cumberland doesn't want ransom. He wants the throne.'

'The British people wouldn't have a murderer on the throne.'

'Unless he made it look like the work of someone else.'

'That's possible,' Blackstone said. 'Do I have your permission to follow up my theory?'

Birnie said: 'You're supposed to be suspended.'

'Perhaps you would consider lifting my suspension if I found the future Queen of England.'

'I might.'

Blackstone thought he noticed a smile on Birnie's face; he couldn't be sure – you had to be quick with Birnie's smiles.

Blackstone said: 'Just ask them for a little grace. Until tonight – as late as you can make it. Tell them to keep the news quiet till then. If you're right and the motives behind this are more complicated than ransom, the kidnappers will want the world to know that the Princess is missing. That must be their whole purpose. If I can get her back by tonight then we might be able to keep it a secret. After all, who really knows? The Duchess, Fräulein Lehzen, you and me and Page and one or two ministers. If the news never gets out then we've defeated whoever's behind all this.'

'Liverpool doesn't want the news to get out either,' Birnie said.

'There you are, sir. And I'm damn sure Peel doesn't either.'

'Nor would Canning,' Birnie said. 'If we can't safeguard our own heir to the throne what authority can we have in Europe?'

'Do I have your permission?'

'I can't stop you,' Birnie said. 'Short of arresting you.'

'Thank you,' Blackstone said.

'I wonder which of us has the bigger task,' Birnie said.

Blackstone thought of the Carthusians, Harrovians and Etonians awaiting Birnie; Liverpool, Peel and Canning, all with Christ Church behind them. 'I think you have, sir.'

He wished for Poacher, but the borrowed grey would have to do. It galloped well as if it sensed the urgency. He rode fiercely, and the outskirts of London, sparkling with hoar frost, fled behind them.

Half a mile from the turnpike he slowed to a canter. Somewhere here Challoner had changed carriage and horses. It was the right place and it was where he would have done it. The fields were calm and white, holly bushes scarlet with berries – it was going to be a hard winter.

A lane led off to the right. He slowed to a trot, stopped altogether. The breath of horse and rider steamed on the sharp air.

As far as he could remember, having been here once on a murder when an old couple had been bludgeoned to death for the few pounds sewn into their mattress, there were no more turnings before the turnpike. This was the logical place. This is where I would have gone. The quest was a lust. Challoner, where are you?

He turned the horse down the lane towards the white farmhouse with the Tudor beams.

There was no one at home. But the house had a lived-in air about it with the frost thawed at the base of the walls as if fires had recently been alight.

Blackstone noticed a shed stuffed with hay. It looked as if it had been stacked in a slipshod fashion within the past few days.

He went round the back looking for the occupants. Behind the house was a kitchen garden. It had a neglected air about it, with a few runner beans still hanging from the dying stalks; at the end someone had been digging with a pick-axe to penetrate the frost.

Beyond the garden was a copse. He walked through it, the scent of the quarry strong in his nostrils. He pushed his way through some brambles and came to some stables. But they were empty and the doors were open.

Ahead lay fields, melting in patches in the uncertain sunlight. The horses stood in one corner of a field, nuzzling together for warmth. All except two which stood apart as if ostracized.

He walked towards them. But a man appeared from the copse carrying a blunderbuss. He aimed the gun and shouted at Blackstone.

Blackstone stopped and waited.

The man came up to him. He had polished cheeks and the sort of cruelty in his expression that is peculiar to some countrymen. The sort of man who would have resented the banning of man-traps.

He prodded the muzzle of the gun at Blackstone's stomach. 'What are you doing on my land?'

Blackstone said: 'Looking for two horses.'

'What horses? What are you talking about? You're lucky I didn't shoot you first and ask questions later.'

'You're lucky you didn't.' He showed the man his baton. 'Bow Street Runner. Edmund Blackstone. There are a few questions I want to ask you.'

The man waved the gun around, but it had lost its power: it was no longer the extension of the man that a gun has to be. 'What questions?'

'Those horses over there.' He pointed at the ostracized animals, one black and one with a blaze on its forehead. 'Who owns them?'

The man looked and Blackstone took the blunderbuss off him in one movement.

The man shouted and lunged forward. But he was cumbersome, spongy with cider. Blackstone stepped back and stuck the blunderbuss in the man's gut; it sank in a couple of inches. 'Those horses,' he said, 'who do they belong to?'

'They're mine.'

'Don't lie.' Another prod with the gun. 'I don't want to

shoot you. Not with your own gun, anyway. But it's very different from you shooting me. If I pull the trigger no questions will be asked.' (Well, only a few.) 'Now, who do they belong to?'

'They're mine,' the man said, finding the second-wind common to cowards before total collapse.

'I see. In that case I must warn you that they've been involved in a very serious crime. The most serious crime of the century. If they're yours you're an accessory. And you'll be hanged.'

'I don't know what you're talking about.'

'Turn around.'

The man turned.

'What's your name?'

'Manston,' said the man.

'All right, Manston. Back to the house.' Half way back he asked: 'Did you know what those horses were used for?'

'No,' Manston said.

'They're your horses and you don't know what they were used for?'

'I don't know what you're talking about.'

They reached the end of the kitchen garden. Why should a man dig in a neglected plot with a pick-axe? 'Stop,' Blackstone said. He picked up a fork and stuck it into the disturbed earth, holding the blunderbuss in his free hand. He put one foot on the shoulder of the fork and raised it as a man raises potatoes. Except that he raised the ruined head of Harry Malt.

'You'd better tell me everything,' Blackstone said, when they were sitting in the farmhouse beside the cold ashes of the fire.

'I didn't kill him.'

'Who did?'

'Henry Challoner.'

It all poured out like ice suddenly melted.

'What did he pay you?'

'£50.'

Blackstone expressed surprise. 'That's a lot of money. You knew it was a big job?'

'I knew that, yes.'

'What did Challoner tell you the job was?'

'A kidnap.'

'But you didn't know who he intended to kidnap?'

'No, I swear it.'

'I don't believe you, Manston.'

Men like Manston, he reflected, always retained one lie. It was a question of self-respect. It had no bearing on the destiny already written; it was a last boast before the gallows.

Manston said: 'I knew it was a kidnap. That's all.'

'And you didn't recognize the girl?'

'No.'

Blackstone's voice was soft. 'Manston, I want to tell you a few things. You are an accessory to the kidnap of the Princess Alexandrina Victoria. The proof is in your fields – the two horses. In addition you are involved in the murder of the man known as Harry Malt. One way and another you seem destined for the gallows.'

Manston abandoned self-respect. He was shivering like a man pulled from a frozen lake. 'No,' he said. 'No.'

'Yes,' Blackstone said.

'Is there anything . . .?'

'Yes,' Blackstone said. 'If you think a little harder and tell me *everything* you know, then there's a chance for you. Just a chance. No more.' He jerked the blunderbuss.

Manston said: 'Challoner came to see me about a month ago. He said he wanted to use my farm as a coaching station for a little while. I was to look after the horses and hide the carriage and have another one waiting. He provided the other carriage as well. He offered me £25 and I said it wasn't enough. So he doubled it. Just like that. It's been a bad harvest and I just couldn't resist . . .'

'Where's the other carriage?'

'In the barn. Under all that hay.'

They went to the barn where Blackstone pulled the hay away. There was the black carriage, lithe and fast beneath its mud. The Runners might be able to trace its owner, Blackstone thought; but, knowing Challoner, it probably wouldn't lead them anywhere. Or would it? He peered at the door. Some sort of pattern had been scratched away. Blackstone didn't doubt that, under close examination, it would prove to be the Cumberland coat-of-arms.

They went back into the house.

Blackstone asked: 'Did Challoner give you an address?'

'He told me of an inn near Wapping where he could be contacted. The Angel.'

'Did he say where he was taking the child?'

Manston shook his head.

'Are you sure?'

'On my life. I asked him but he told me to mind my own business. I didn't want to know anyway.'

'Was it near here?'

'Perhaps. I don't know. You'd better ask the pikeman.'

'I presume he was an accessory?'

'He was that all right.'

'Bradley, isn't it?'

'That's right,' Manston said. 'How did you know?'

'I know all the keepers. Especially Bradley.' He stood up. 'I'll need another horse, Manston. You'll give it to me.' He poked around in the ashes looking for a little heat; he found a glowing ember that died at once. 'By the way, where's your wife?'

'She had nothing to do with it.' Manston began to tremble again.

'Don't jest with me,' Blackstone said. 'Get her up. I want some breakfast.' He jerked the gun again. 'Why are you so scared on behalf of your wife? We both know she was involved. She had to be. Is it the money, Manston? Didn't you tell her you were getting £50?'

'It's not that.'

'What is it then?'

'The killing,' Manston whispered. 'I didn't tell her about the killing.'

Blackstone ate pigeon pie, ham, eggs and muffins washed down with brown stout. 'You don't live too badly,' he told Manston, while Mrs Manston hovered in the kitchen, as pale as her husband was red.

'We manage,' Manston said.

'And the men who work for you. . . . How do they manage?'

'They're among the best paid labourers in the country.'

'What do they get – £5 a year?'

'More than that,' Manston said.

'Then they're lucky. And today they're going to be even luckier. Because you, Manston, are going to distribute your £50 to them. Christmas will be here soon and they'll be very glad of it.'

'No.' There was anguish in Manston's voice. 'I took risks. . . . Perhaps you would like a little of the money. Say £5, £10 . . .'

Blackstone put down his knife and fork. 'Distribute it, Manston. I'll be coming back this way soon. I hope to find a lot of labourers in a very grateful frame of mind towards their employer.' He stood up. 'The alternative is the gallows.'

From the kitchen came a cry of horror.

Blackstone went on: 'And don't make the mistake of running away. You won't get far and before nightfall every parish constable, every horse patrol and half the Army will be looking for you.'

Outside, a new horse, a sensitive-looking chestnut, was tethered to the post. Blackstone spoke to it for a few moments, stroking its neck. He hoped they would understand each other. Then he mounted.

'Better get back to your digging, Manston,' he said, and rode off to the turnpike.

The toll houses of the turnpike stood on either side of the road. They were squat and stone-built, linked across the road by two long gates.

Bradley, the pikeman, was a small man who walked with a stoop; but he had been a coal miner and his shoulders were powerful, the sort called upon to support collapsing tunnels. His face was hard, with scar tissue still imprisoning specks of coal dust, and at the same time sly; he looked around him as if daylight were still a surprise.

He wore a tall black glazed hat, corduroy breeches, white stockings and a white linen apron. But the young bloods who like to fight a pikeman for the tolls didn't often manage to knock the hat from his head: his apprenticeship in brawling had been thorough.

He had worked at the turnpike for three years and had been given a horse so that he could work closely with the horse patrols. Blackstone knew that he also worked closely with criminals.

He found him polishing his silver.

'Blackie,' Bradley said, 'what a surprise.' He had a good northern rasp to his voice which contradicted his furtive manner.

Blackstone sat down and pointed to the silver. 'I see you're investing your money sensibly, Bradley.'

'The odd piece of plate here and there, Blackie.'

'You should have hidden it before I arrived.'

'I didn't know you were coming.' He laughed uncertainly. 'What brings you here, Blackie?'

Blackstone picked up a silver goblet. 'Very nice too, Bradley. Could it have been stolen from the Star Hotel, Southampton?'

'No, Blackie, not that one. Is that what you're looking for – swag?'

Blackstone detected hope. He shook his head.

Bradley gave the goblet a final rub with a blackened rag. 'What are you after then?'

'What have you done with the £50, Bradley? It's a lot of money for you.'

'What £50?'

Blackstone leaned across the table scattered with plate, most of it stolen. 'I haven't much time, Bradley. I don't want a long argument. I know you were paid £50 to say you hadn't seen Challoner pass through here in a carriage.' He watched for reaction. 'And to say you hadn't seen a child in the carriage.'

'I don't know what you're talking about, Blackie.'

Blackstone sighed. 'Weren't you questioned last night?'

'I wouldn't call it questioning. After all I work *with* the law not against it. The horse patrol asked if I'd seen a black carriage pass by with a child inside it. That's all. But I hadn't seen any such carriage, Blackie.'

'I know,' Blackstone said. 'You were telling the truth, weren't you? Because we both know it was a blue and maroon carriage.'

'I don't know anything about a blue and maroon carriage.'

'Do you know who was in that carriage, Bradley?'

'I've already told you, Blackie. I didn't see any such carriage.'

'Princess Alexandrina Victoria.' He reminded Bradley about the gallows, about the possibility of being hanged, drawn and quartered.

Bradley tried to speak as if they shared the *camaraderie* of the law. 'Don't try and scare me of all people, Blackie.' He attempted a laugh. 'Do you remember that murder you worked on here a few years ago? You really got the locals frightened that time.'

'Two old people murdered for a few pounds? What did they expect? They were hiding someone. I knew it and they knew I knew it.'

'But you caught him, didn't you, Blackie? And got his neck stretched for him.'

Blackstone let him digress hopefully for a few minutes, then said: 'The carriage, Bradley. Where was it going?'

'Come off it, Blackie.'

Blackstone stood up, pocket pistol in hand. 'I've got two alternatives, Bradley. Either to beat the truth out of you or take you back to Bow Street.'

'You'd need a warrant . . .' Bradley began.

'It wouldn't be the first time I've taken a man in without a warrant.' Blackstone picked up some of the plate. 'And this is stolen property, Bradley.'

Bradley went for the gun he kept in a drawer under the table.

Blackstone hit his knuckle with the butt of his pistol. He opened the drawer and took out the gun – a .68 French holster pistol, too big for clever work under tables.

Blackstone said: 'I'm taking you back to Bow Street, Bradley.' He tossed the French pistol into a corner of the room. 'A turnpike keeper receiving swag? Hanging or transportation. Now let's get your horse and ride to London.'

Bradley examined his bleeding knuckle. 'It's broken,' he said. 'You've broken my hand.'

'Also,' Blackstone told him, 'I have a statement from a witness directly implicating you in the kidnapping of the heir to the throne of England. For that misdemeanour, Bradley, the crowd would probably be allowed to tear you apart alive.'

Bradley sucked his knuckles. 'If I was to help you, Blackie . . .'

'You'd better be quick,' Blackstone said. 'First, where's the money?'

Bradley took some money out of the drawer and tossed it on the table.

Blackstone counted it. 'And the rest, Bradley.'

'That's the lot, Blackie.'

'And the rest, Bradley. You got £50 for this job. There's only twenty-five sovereigns here.'

Bradley fetched the balance from a kitchen drawer. 'I was going to hide it today,' he said.

Blackstone prodded him back to the chair. 'Now, tell me about the carriage. And about Challoner.'

'Will you let me off if I do?'

'I don't promise you anything, Bradley. I don't make promises to people like you. But if you don't tell me everything then I'll see you at the gallows.'

Bradley shaded his eyes against the sun which had borrowed a diamond brightness from the frost. Challoner, he said, had approached him about three weeks ago. For £50 he had to do practically nothing. Just turn a blind eye to a blue and maroon carriage and not bother to look inside. In fact he didn't even have to lie because he would be asked about a black carriage.

£50 for that. . . . Bradley pleaded with Blackstone. 'Such easy brass, Blackie. You understand, don't you? I mean you weren't always on the side of the law, were you? Wouldn't you have done the same for £50 in those days?'

Bradley wasn't the first criminal to make this point to Blackstone. Blackstone had made it to himself many times as he arrested a man who had robbed to keep his family from starving. On a few occasions he had let the man go.

He said: 'We're talking about *these* days, Bradley. Not *those* days.'

But Bradley had seen weakness. '£50, Blackie, for doing nothing.'

'There was a child in there,' Blackstone said. 'And you knew it.'

'I didn't know it was the Princess.'

'But you knew it was a child.'

'I didn't think she'd come to any harm. . . .'

Blackstone hardened. 'Where were they going, Bradley?'

'I don't know. On my life I don't know. On my mother's grave. On the Holy Bible.'

'Be quiet,' Blackstone said. Bradley was telling the truth now. So where did he go from here? 'Think back,' he told Bradley. 'Think back to the first time you saw Challoner. Where did he come from? And did he say where he was going then?'

'He was with a man called Charlston,' Bradley said.

Blackstone asked: 'Which direction did they come from?'

'From the north,' Bradley said. Hesitantly he added: 'I seem to remember them saying something about a house two hours' ride from here.'

'And there's only one road north from here?'

Bradley nodded.

Blackstone said: 'You may have saved yourself from the gallows. But don't bet on it.' He picked up the money. 'Don't spend this, Bradley. Farmer Manston has a plan for distributing funds to his workers. This will come in handy.'

He went outside and mounted the horse. As he rode north he found he was thinking more about Challoner than the Princess.

Chapter Three

FROM his side of the long polished table – the junior side – Sir Richard Birnie surveyed and assessed the enemy.

Robert Peel. Home Secretary. Harrow and Christ Church. Only in his thirties but already with Under-Secretary of War and Colonies and the Chief Secretary of Ireland under his belt. Now directing his genius towards legal reform and the establishment of a Metropolitan Police Force. A zealot, in Birnie's opinion. But a plausible and relentless zealot. Such a chilling exterior; and yet they said he felt pain more than most people, such was his sensitivity. A friend of the poet Lord Byron who had died two years earlier giving his support to the Greeks trying to overthrow the Turks. Birnie sometimes wished that the duel between Peel and O'Connell in Ostend hadn't been stopped by the arrest of the Irishman. Who knows. . . .

At the head of the table sat the Prime Minister, Lord Liverpool – Robert Banks Jenkinson. Charterhouse and Christ Church. A solid man they said – with faint praise. A man of unfailing temper. But he stayed, and stayed, despite the running fight with the Prince of Wales, now George IV, despite Ireland, despite bad health.

Also present: George Canning, Foreign Minister, orator, poet, actor, Eton and Christ Church, and Arthur Wellesley, the Duke of Wellington, who had just returned from St Petersburg where he had been congratulating Tsar Nicholas on his accession. Wellington, Master General of the Ordnance, was the only man present with whom Birnie felt any rapport; he admired the nerve and the strength of will, tempered by caution, of the hero of Waterloo. It was unfortunate that Birnie was sitting on Wellington's deaf side.

Birnie didn't at first contribute much. The birthright and scholarship assembled here at No. 10 Downing Street affected him so that he heard himself speaking. He was under attack and he answered the questions as briefly as possible. He was not overawed by the ministers: self-consciousness did not necessarily interfere with resolution. And around him he sensed indecision.

Liverpool was speaking. Solidly but cautiously. 'What we should do, gentlemen, is alert every military unit, every magistrate, every parish constable, every foot and horse patrol, every watchman, and tell them that the Princess has been abducted.'

Birnie noted the emphasis on *should*, and waited.

Canning asked: 'What will the world think of us if we're incapable even of safeguarding our own Royalty?'

'I don't think,' Peel said carefully, 'that we should put our international reputation before the safety of the future Queen.'

Wellington, his hand cupped to his good ear, said: 'Peel is right. None of us is in any doubt that this is a national emergency and we must mobilize every force possible.' He swung round disconcertingly to Birnie. 'What do you think, Sir Richard?'

'It seems to me,' Birnie said, listening to himself, 'that the safety of the Princess must surely prevail.'

'There are some who would disagree with you,' Peel said.

'You mean Cumberland?' the Prime Minister asked.

'And his supporters.'

'It's difficult to believe that he has any.'

'Not so difficult. If we presume that his supporters are also the conspirators who have kidnapped the Princess then they would be the favourites at the court of King Ernest.'

Wellington rubbed his big foraging nose and said: 'If that man became King of England I would personally put him to the sword.'

'I thought,' Canning observed, 'that your greatest fear was civil war in England.'

'That, sir,' Wellington said, 'is my second greatest fear. The first would be seeing the Duke of Cumberland on the throne of England.' He stared meditatively at Canning whose brilliant strokes of diplomacy might well conceal instability.

Liverpool aimed a few even-tempered words at Birnie. 'I'm afraid that at some stage, Sir Richard, we shall have to hold an inquiry into the circumstances under which the abduction was permitted to happen.'

'I understand that, sir.' Birnie paused for delicate emphasis. 'I'm sure that the Home Secretary will have the question of responsibility in mind.'

Thoughtfully, Peel said that he would.

'The responsibility being that of the Home Secretary,' Canning observed. 'It does seem to me that precautions were minimal in view of the fears expressed by the Duchess of Kent that an attempt might be made to abduct the Princess.'

'Fears expressed by one neurotic woman,' Peel said.

Birnie struck swiftly. 'I'm glad that the Home Secretary recalls the original feeling about the Duchess's fears and the lack of urgency about the investigation.'

The mind of the man who got a double first in classics and mathematics turned itself on Birnie. Peel said: 'A certain Edmund Blackstone was assigned to the job. A Bow Street Runner of some repute. It has been puzzling me why he was removed and this man Page was substituted.'

Liverpool stopped them. 'It's not the time for recriminations. We have to decide what to do.'

Wellington turned again to Birnie. 'I feel, sir, that you are talking with some reservation. As if perhaps you have a plan?'

'Not exactly a plan, Your Grace.' He stopped listening to himself and his Scots accent returned. 'But it seems to me that a general alert might jeopardize the life of the Princess. If her captors hear that the Army is galloping down the road they might murder her so that she can't identify them and then make good their escape. I also feel that those behind this kidnap are anxious that the world should know. If we can keep it secret for a little longer then it might be to everyone's advantage. Including the Princess's.'

'But only if there's any chance of finding her,' Liverpool said. 'Do you think there's any chance, Sir Richard?'

'There is a chance,' Birnie said.

'Then what is it, for God's sake?' Peel asked. 'You've kept very quiet about this, Sir Richard. . . .'

'I wanted to hear the views of the Government first,' Birnie told him. 'I was interested in the question of responsibility. . . .'

'That's simple,' Peel said. 'The Bow Street Runners were assigned to the job. The protection of the Monarchy has long been their responsibility.'

'I think,' Wellington said, 'that you just admitted that the original fears were not taken too seriously. . . .'

Liverpool held up his hand. 'Please, gentlemen.'

Birnie said: 'Supposing the Bow Street Runners were to find the Princess?'

'Then their future would be assured for the next hundred years,' Canning said.

'I wasn't aware,' Liverpool said, 'that their future was in any doubt.'

Birnie and Peel looked at each other.

Wellington said: 'Are you telling us, Sir Richard, that the Bow Street Runners can find the Princess?'

Birnie allowed himself another significant pause. 'It's possible.'

Liverpool said: 'Please enlighten us, Sir Richard.'

Birnie told them about Blackstone.

'The man you took off the assignment,' Peel said after he had finished.

'The best man we have.'

'What about Townsend?'

'He's getting old.'

The Prime Minister said: 'How long does this man Blackstone want?'

Birnie told them that Blackstone hoped to have news by nightfall – although he might not be able to relay it immediately.

They all thought about it and Birnie heard their thoughts. About responsibility. About provoking civil war. About the authority of Britain abroad.

Finally Liverpool said: 'What concerns me – and, I'm sure, everyone here – is the safety of the Princess. It does seem to me that a general alert might further endanger her. But we cannot delay for long. If this man Blackstone succeeds then the world need never know. I know that none of you gentlemen' – he gestured with a dry veiny hand – 'would ever disclose this secret. And I'm sure that all those who know about what has happened could be persuaded. This man Blackstone. His colleague Page.' He allowed himself a smile. 'I'm sure Mr Page wouldn't object to total secrecy. Obviously the Duchess of Kent and Fräulein Lehzen could be convinced of the wisdom of keeping quiet in the interests of the Princess. We should tell them,' he explained, 'that once a crime has been made public there is invariably an imitative venture. I understand that the staff at Kensington Palace is unaware so far of what has occurred. They have been told that the Princess is indisposed and is confined to her room. So, whom does that leave?'

Peel said: 'Sir John Conroy.'

'Ah yes,' Liverpool said. 'Sir John. I don't think we need have any fears in that direction. He is, after all, very close to the Duchess and the Princess. I am quite sure that he would appreciate the wisdom of discretion.'

'With respect,' Canning said, 'you seem to be forgetting one other person. You seem to be forgetting the Princess herself. She must be told to forget that she was ever kidnapped. Rather a tall order, isn't it?'

'I don't think so,' Liverpool said. 'She is only a little girl but she shows great acumen. If we ask her to forget then she will do her best. She has about her a regal appreciation of what might one day be required of her. It's almost as if she knew what the future holds for her. I feel she would understand even if she had to keep it out of her diaries. Carry the secret to her grave if needs be.'

'Which could be today,' Peel said.

'Do you have any other suggestions?' Liverpool asked.

Peel stood up. 'I think,' he said, 'that we should proceed along the lines suggested by Sir Richard. But only until tonight. If Edmund Blackstone hasn't found her by then we must scour the country until she is found.' He turned to Birnie. 'I hope your trust in this man Blackstone is well founded, Sir Richard. Perhaps at some later date you might be so good as to tell me why he was taken off the assignment.'

Birnie accepted the ultimatum.

If Blackstone failed then everything was the responsibility of Bow Street.

He felt his age sagging on his face, weighting the pouches under his eyes.

He said: 'I have every faith in Blackstone.'

Liverpool said: 'Then is it agreed, gentlemen?'

Canning said it was. Wellington said it was after Liverpool had repeated the words into his right ear. Peel said it was, the personal ultimatum still implied in his voice.

The Prime Minister said: 'Then we shall meet again tonight, gentlemen. Ten o'clock?' It was an order.

Peel said: 'And if we have heard nothing by then. . . .'

Birnie said: 'Then the Bow Street Runners have failed.'

Life, he thought, was an ultimatum.

A few miles away, Lawler, conducting his inquiries below the stairs at Kensington Palace, made three discoveries which he decided should be communicated to Blackstone.

The first discovery surfaced in bed with Mary Singleton.

She asked him: 'Do you love me, Lawler?'

Lawler said he did.

She sighed luxuriously. 'When shall we get married?'

'Soon,' Lawler said.

'How soon. Let's make it a definite date.'

Lawler kissed her. But when he stopped, her greedy eyes, always on the lookout for biscuits, were regarding him suspiciously.

'You're not married, are you?'

'No.' Lawler shook his head vehemently.

'Are you sure?'

'I'm not married I tell you.'

She relaxed, pulling the sheet across her large breasts. 'Oh Lawler,' she sighed. Then asked for the first time: 'What's your first name?'

'I haven't got one,' Lawler said. 'I've always been called Lawler until they made me John the footman. Isn't Lawler good enough?'

'I suppose so,' she said. 'But how will we get on at the marriage ceremony, you only having one name?'

'I don't know,' Lawler said, wondering if he should get out now. But Blackstone had asked him to stay. Blackstone was in trouble and seemed to be relying on Lawler to help him. It was the first time that anything resembling trust had been placed in Lawler.

Mary Singleton said: 'This is wonderful, Lawler, isn't it? No work to do and just the two of us together here.'

Lawler, who had an appointment in half an hour with Irma, said: 'What do you mean – no work to do?'

'Didn't you know? The Princess is ill again. And no one must go into the room except her mother and Fräulein Lehzen. They don't seem to trust the English. But it's a bit odd, isn't it?'

Lawler, who had been working that day in another part of the Palace until returning to Mary Singleton's authority, agreed that it was odd. Very odd, he thought. But at least it gave him some leisure to make his inquiries. After a while he told her that he had to see the house steward.

In the little room inhabited by Irma the chime of the clock above the fireplace sounded to Lawler like more wedding bells.

He sat beside the bed and poured himself a glass of Madeira

from a bottle stolen from the butler's pantry. He would have preferred a few pints of stout to replenish his virility; but Madeira was better than nothing.

Irma sat expectantly on the edge of the bed. A cottage in Camberwell would be nice, she told him.

Lawler wondered if he had missed his vocation. He seemed to do rather better with women than horses. But what was the penalty for bigamy? With luck it might be transportation.

He poured himself more Madeira and asked: 'What's the gossip today?'

'This and that,' she said, smiling, her teeth very white and even in her dairy face.

'I hear the Princess is ill again.'

'Yes, poor little thing. Locked in her room with those Germans.' She spoke as if the Germans might be infectious.

'What's wrong with her?'

'No one seems to know.'

'Can't you find out?'

'Why would you want to know?'

Lawler shrugged. 'I don't really.' He stretched and gauged the time element: Irma had fifteen minutes before she was required by Lady Jane Hatherley. 'Been in the still-room lately?' he asked.

'Oh, for heaven's sake.' She flounced herself back on the bed.

'What's the matter?'

'You're the most unromantic man I've ever known.'

'We met in the still-room, didn't we?'

'I suppose so.' She softened. 'I thought you were very bold.'

'And a little below your station?'

'Oh no, Lawler, I never thought that.'

He poured more Madeira and, holding the glass in one hand, slipped the other round her waist. 'It was a funny old meeting, wasn't it?'

'You asked me about the laudanum. I thought that was strange.'

'Any missing since?' Lawler asked casually.

She shook her head. 'None. Why do you keep on about laudanum?' She wriggled closer to him. 'Give us an old kiss, Lawler.'

After a few kisses, during which Lawler glanced at his watch a couple of times to remind her that there was no time for any developments, he asked her again about the gossip.

'Oh, nothing very much,' she said, straightening her uniform. 'But I think Lady Jane's a bit sweet on that fellow Blackstone. Mind you, I don't blame her. He's the only real man they've had in the Palace since I came here.' She touched his hand. 'Except you, of course.'

Lawler was interested. 'Why do you think she's sweet on him?'

'Because I found a letter she was writing to him. He's been dismissed, you know. Something to do with beating one of the grooms.'

'Yes,' Lawler told her, 'I had heard that.' He tried to pour another glass of Madeira but the bottle was empty. 'What did she say to him?'

'You're very nosey, my love.'

'I have an inquiring mind.'

'That's the same thing, isn't it?' She looked at the clock. 'Heavens, I must fly.'

Lawler put both arms round her waist. 'What did she say?'

'Oh, nothing much. I didn't have time to read it properly. She was apologizing for something. And there was a lot about Sir Rupert Charlston in it. That was sad, wasn't it, about Sir Rupert?'

'Not very,' Lawler said. 'What else did she say?'

'Not much else. She hadn't finished writing it. But what she had written seemed very affectionate. . . .'

'God help her,' Lawler said without thinking.

'Why do you say that?'

'He doesn't look the sort of man who would be faithful to one woman, that's all.'

'Funny,' she said, 'I got the impression that you knew him or something.'

Lawler managed a laugh. 'I don't know any Bow Street Runners.'

'Then why were you asking me about the missing miniature?'

'I thought we might be able to get something going ourselves.'

'What sort of thing, Lawler?'

'Well, we didn't pinch it, did we? So if we happened to find it we might get a reward for it. Or we might even be able to suggest to whoever stole it that we might keep quiet if he liked to help us out a bit.'

'You mean blackmail? Oh Lawler!' There was shock and admiration in her voice.

'Have you heard anything about it?'

'Not a thing.' She put on her white apron and tucked her hair into her cap.

'Well, keep your eyes open.' He went to the door. 'Was that the only gossip you had?'

'I told you it wasn't much. There's a bit of talk about Sir John Conroy flirting with the Duchess – before the Princess's illness. And with the Princess Sophie. One of the housemaids saw him kissing the Duchess apparently. But you're not interested in that sort of thing, are you, Lawler?'

Lawler said he wasn't. She gave him a kiss before he left. More of a seal than a sign of affection.

Much later he made his way to the room of Amy Hucklestone, who had arrived at the Palace, he had learned, through the endeavours of the London Society for the Encouragement of Faithful Female Servants, an association founded by the Rev. H. G. Watkins to 'promote mutual tenderness, good will and confidence among the superior and subordinate branches of a family; and to secure the young and unwary but virtuous female from the danger of resorting to common registry offices'.

Lawler thought that Amy was a little too influenced by Mr Watkins's emphasis on virtue. On the other hand he respected her for it; it was also a relief from the rigours of the other two girls.

He knocked at her door and she asked him what he wanted. 'Just a chat,' he said.

'You shouldn't come here, you know.'

'You're right,' Lawler said.

'Perhaps just for a minute,' Amy said hastily.

The room contained a narrow bed beside a small window. Above the bed was a bookshelf bearing an old copy of *Pamela*, some 6d plays, a copy of Biddulph's 'Prayers for the Morning and Evening of Every Day Through the Week', and a Bible propped up at one end by an enamel box bearing a picture of the Pavilion at Brighton. Above the books was a print of the Crucifixion; at the end of the bed Amy's box. Lawler wondered what it contained.

'You really shouldn't be here,' Amy said.

But she shut the door and Lawler wondered if he had been wrong about Amy. 'Then why are you letting me in?'

'I'll tell you why,' she said. 'Because I could do with a laugh, that's why.'

'What's the matter?' he asked. 'Here' – he handed her his handkerchief – 'don't cry.'

'I'm sorry.' She dabbed at the tears assembling in the corners of her eyes. 'But I get so fed up with everything. And I can't see it ever changing. There'll always be two different sorts of people – the rich and us. Just because of the way we were born ...'

'Has something special happened today?'

'Nothing so special. I broke a plate while I was dusting. I didn't have to own up. It was only a chip and it could have been years before anyone spotted it. But Mr Watkins told us always to tell the truth about breakages. He said most employers would forgive you if you owned up.' She paused significantly. 'Not here they don't.'

'You mean they punished you for it?'

'The housekeeper said I'd have to pay a part of the cost out of my own money.'

'Miserable sods,' Lawler said.

'What's the point of honesty?' Amy asked as the tears took up position again.

Lawler, who had never seen much point to it, kept quiet.

Amy said: 'Do you think I should have confessed to breaking the plate?'

'It's a difficult question to answer with an honest girl like yourself. You see, I never had any Rev. Watkins to preach to me.'

'Are you a dishonest man then?'

Lawler wished keenly for a change of subject. 'None of us is perfect,' he said.

'You seem so different to the others here.'

'It's just that I haven't been used to Royal households.'

'Why should that make any difference?'

'I don't know.'

Lawler wished he could make her laugh. But he didn't want to become a song-and-dance man in her presence. That was the effect she had on him. Odd, because she enjoyed his company and he made her laugh.

Amy said: 'You're not going to stay here, are you?'

'What makes you say that?' He looked at her sharply.

'I don't know. I think I can tell. You don't seem to have settled like the others. You make this place seem more like a prison than it did before. You know – as if you're just waiting to escape. To get beyond those trees.' She pointed out of the small window at the branches beckoning in the night. 'I've never been so unsettled before,' she said. 'That Mr Blackstone started it.'

'Why?' Lawler asked. 'What did he do?'

'Do? He didn't *do* anything. He was just kind, that's all. Not like the others. Not,' she added, 'that they're all unkind. It's just that they don't think. They don't seem to regard us as human beings at all, do they, Lawler?'

Perhaps a joke would help. But he couldn't think of any. 'Do we regard them as human beings?' he asked.

'We're all the same in God's eyes.'

'Ah yes,' Lawler said. 'So we are.' He glanced at the Bible and Biddulph's prayers. 'Are you very religious, Amy?'

The tears had dried. 'Not really,' she confessed. 'You know, I go to church sometimes. But you couldn't really say I was religious. Not really.'

Lawler was thankful. 'What do you like doing? Apart from breaking plates, that is.'

He was rewarded by a laugh. 'I like to go down to Vauxhall,' she told him. 'Or to the Tower. I went to the theatre once.'

'When's your next day off?'

'In two weeks' time,' Amy said.

'Perhaps we might go up to town together,' Lawler suggested.

On the wall, just to the right of the Crucifixion, a bell jangled.

Amy said: 'I'm wanted downstairs.'

'Let them wait.'

'I can't do that. I'm in enough trouble already.'

'All right,' Lawler said. 'I'll wait here.'

'No, you'd better not.'

But Lawler felt more sure of himself now because she hadn't turned him down. He reached for Biddulph's prayers, sat down beside the bed and crossed his legs. 'I'll just make myself at home with Mr Biddulph.'

'I don't think . . .' The bell jangled again. 'I'll have to go. . .' She looked flustered.

'And I'll be here when you come back. Don't worry – I won't pry into your secrets.'

When she had gone he put the book down and circled the room. He wasn't tall but his head brushed the ceiling. Outside the branches of the trees were blacker than the night and the courtyards were lacquered silver by the moonlight. But there was nothing soft about the light: there was a blade in this night and it made Lawler uneasy. It summoned other nights from the past, hungry nights before he had made a bit of money taking bets and doing jobs for Blackstone.

He perused this night for a while hoping to find velvet in

it: but it didn't relent. He pulled the darned, pink curtains. They made him feel sad about the broken plate. For God's sake, what was happening to him? He was tired of being John the footman. He wanted his sporting prints, the thrush singing in the corner. To hell with Blackstone, he decided. But he had decided that before.

He went to replace the prayers on the shelf above the bed. But as he did so old instincts from youthful excursions into burglary stirred. He stared with fascination at the loose brick just showing behind the Bible. There was sweat on his palms and he was aware of the quickening of his heart. He removed the brick and took out the missing miniature.

Then he sat down and laughed helplessly. He was still laughing when Amy Hucklestone came back.

'You,' he said, still laughing.

'You had no right . . .'

'I had no right? That's good, Amy. That's very good indeed.'

'What sort of man are you to pry around in my bedroom. Looking behind the Holy Bible.'

Lawler began to laugh again – the sort of laughter that incapacitates you in the classroom. 'Looking behind the Holy Bible,' he managed. 'Oh Lor!' When he had recovered himself a little he said: 'Who put it behind the Holy Bible? That's what I'd like to know. Who put it there?'

'I did,' said Amy Hucklestone.

'Why, Amy?' he asked. 'Why?' He noted with relief that she didn't look as if she were going to cry again.

She made her Confession to Lawler the priest. 'It was a day just like this. I'd been working hard lighting the fires, cleaning the doorsteps – cleaning the wallpaper with stale bread, I remember. I was feeling very tired and there was a pain in my knees as if they were going to swell up. You know how they do with some girls. There's some mistresses who get rid of you if you keep getting bad knees. You know how some of them are, Lawler. The sort who turn the gas out at night so's

157

you can't read in bed; the sort who mark the cutlery *Stolen from such and such a place* so's no one can pinch it.'

Lawler was interested. 'I didn't know they did that, Amy.'

'Oh yes,' she said, still not crying. 'There's a lot like that. The sort that keep a lady's-maid – not that I've much time for them – on their feet for sixteen hours a day and then make them stay up a few hours extra when there's a ball on just so that they can undo a few buttons and bows when my lady returns.'

'So why did you steal the miniature?' He thought he might preach to her about dishonesty at any moment.

'I was so tired and my knees were hurting. I wanted to go to bed and sleep because we have to get up at 5.30 in the morning, as you know. But no, another maid was poorly and I had to do the warming-pans. I dropped a hot coal on a rug in one of the bedrooms. I kicked it off but it made a little hole. Just then Fräulein Lehzen came in and kicked up a terrible fuss, saying she would report me to the housekeeper. All of a sudden everything seemed so hopeless. You know, Lawler, the future and everything. What future have we got? Any of us? Dolly-mops, skivvies, drudges for the rest of our lives. . . .'

'I know,' he said. 'I know.' He patted her hand.

'You don't seem very shocked,' she said.

'Oh, but I am. Very deeply shocked.'

'You're being very decent, Lawler.'

'You haven't told me why you pinched it yet.'

'I suppose I had some form of breakdown. I remembered seeing Fräulein Lehzen putting the miniature in a jewel box and yet it was supposed to be missing. I knew it was valuable. I thought to myself, if I could sell it I might get quite a lot of money and perhaps set up a little business somewhere.'

'A girl set up a business?'

'I'm sure there'd be a man somewhere only too happy to help me if I had money.' She paused and looked at Lawler. She sat down on the bed facing him.

Lawler thought: It would be too obvious, dead swag – no

fence would touch it. He also considered his loyalty to Blackstone. 'But the jewel box was forced open,' he said. 'Did you do that?'

She nodded. Quite calm. Facing execution with martyred serenity. 'I used a pair of scissors. I didn't think they would work. I mean, I thought the jewel box would have been stronger than that. But it opened quite easily. I think Fräulein Lehzen should have put the jewel box away in a strong box. But she must have forgotten.'

'What were you going to do with the loot?'

'The what?'

'The miniature. How did you hope to get rid of it?'

'I didn't know. I got in a terrible panic when I got back to my room. Then I remembered noticing the loose brick when I put my books up there. I levered it out with the scissors and dug it out a bit more so there'd be room for the miniature. Then I put the brick back and put the Bible in front of it.'

A nice touch, Lawler thought.

'And I haven't looked at it since. I sort of hoped that it had been spirited away.'

'And now you know it hasn't?'

'I'll take my punishment,' Amy said.

Lawler regarded her with admiration. He had always been suspicious of the honesty in her character. Even now he wasn't sure. Had she stolen the miniature in a bout of hysteria? And just how honest was this particular display of honesty? A suspicion lingered in Lawler's mind that she was arranging for him to become an accomplice. He glanced around the room. The neat frugal possessions. The Bible, the prayers – not necessarily consulted. He thought he was a good judge of character: you had to be, taking bets and laying them. But this girl defeated him.

He said: 'You'd get a long stretch for this.'

'I deserve it.'

'Is it the first time you've pinched anything?'

'Oh Lawler,' she exclaimed. 'Of course it is.' Just the same, she didn't seem too ashamed.

'I'm sorry,' he said.

'What are you going to do? Tell the Bow Street Runner, I suppose.'

'I don't know,' Lawler said.

'I wouldn't have minded so much with that Mr Blackstone.'

Lawler, who was tiring of hearing female admiration for Blackstone, said: 'Why? Because you think he would have let you off? No such luck there, my love.'

'You seem to know a lot about him, Lawler.'

He wished she would cry; her composure was unnatural.

'I just know that a Bow Street Runner wouldn't let you off just like that.'

'So you'll tell this man Page? I don't like him, Lawler, I really don't.'

'Oh for God's sake!' The conversation seemed to be wandering at curious angles. She had pinched the Princess's miniature and yet here they were discussing the merits of Blackstone and Page. He waited for her to reprimand him for blaspheming, but she said nothing.

He said: 'Of course, you could blame the German bitch for leaving the jewel box there when she should have put it in the safe. Also because she went for you like that when all you'd done was drop a red hot coal on the rug.' This struck him as funny and schoolroom laughter began to inflate again. 'Yes,' he decided, 'you could definitely blame Fräulein Lehzen for the whole thing.'

Amy Hucklestone began to laugh. An amazing girl, Amy. 'She should be arrested,' she said.

'Both of you should be arrested,' Lawler said. Which stopped her a bit.

'Are you going to peach on me, Lawler?'

'What, tell the law?'

She nodded.

'I couldn't do that, Amy. I just couldn't. It wouldn't be right.'

'But it would be right.'

'Not where I come from,' Lawler said. 'No, it definitely

wouldn't be right where I come from.' He held her hand. 'But we've got to decide what's to be done.'

'Perhaps,' she said, leaving her hand in his, 'perhaps we could put it back.'

That wouldn't be right either, Lawler thought.

'Too risky,' he said.

'Do you think we should keep it?'

Lawler noted the *we*. He shook his head.

She said: 'I was only thinking about that little business I was talking about. . . .'

'You mean you and me?'

'I don't mean Fräulein Lehzen,' she said.

Laughter overcame them both again.

'No,' he said after a while, 'we couldn't . . . shouldn't go into business on the proceeds of stolen loot. Besides,' he added, 'every nark in England will be on the lookout for that miniature.'

'What should we do then?'

'I'll think of something,' Lawler told her, pocketing the miniature.

'Where are you taking it?'

'Somewhere safer than your hole in the wall.'

She leaned across and kissed him. 'Oh Lawler,' she said.

'Oh Lor' what?'

The laughter more restrained and self-conscious now. So he kissed her and said: 'I'd best be off. It would be a fine old kettle of fish if we were caught here together with the miniature.'

She nodded. 'Be careful.' And then: 'Were you ever a footman, Lawler?'

'Why, don't I act like one?'

'Yes,' she said. 'You *act* like one. But were you ever employed as one?'

She was, he thought, quite shrewd. Such shrewdness was a strange bedmate for honesty. 'I must go now.'

'You didn't answer my question.'

He blew her a kiss, wondering if he was acting the lover now, as he had acted the footman and other parts. He could never be sure.

He paused at the door. 'Interesting about that cutlery marked *Stolen from* . . . Pity they don't do the same with their miniatures.'

'Oh Lawler,' she said.

He opened the door and slipped into the corridor alive with the ticking of the Palace clocks.

Before making contact with Blackstone he had to do one more thing: he had to find out whether the Princess was really ill.

He walked busily down the corridor outside the bedroom where the Duchess of Kent slept with her daughter. It was too early for the Duchess to be in bed; but if the Princess was ill there should at least have been a senior footman on guard. There was no one. He looked up and down the passage and tried the door-handle. The door was locked. Odd.

He walked briskly back puzzling about it. But Blackstone would need more than just a locked door. He always needed more information than Lawler had obtained.

He made his way to the back stairs connecting the two floors on which the family lived. They were dark and narrow and wound up to an oval skylight.

Lawler wished that at least he had a life preserver with him. Instead of a stolen miniature. The ticking of the clocks seemed to have been channelled into the stairway. As if predatory insects were on the march. Pendulum heart-beats and watching eyes.

He reached the top of the stairs and climbed a short step-ladder. He posed there for a moment in the discovering moonlight as if he were on stage. He untied the cord and pushed the skylight up. The staircase gulped the frosty air.

He climbed up on to the roof, imagining his silhouette from the ground, waiting for the warning shout, the crack of a pistol shot. Instead a clock chimed behind him, followed by a hundred other sycophants, each with its own voice and character. Lawler swore softly at them until they stopped. He thought he could still hear the ticking, but it was only his own watch.

He moved slowly along the guttering calling on the clouds to obscure the moon. But the shadowless light remained, incurious and desolate.

When he reached the bedroom skylight he was glad of the moon because there was no light inside. He saw a white-painted French bed with chintz hangings. Empty. The inevitable clock – made from tortoiseshell, his burglar's mind assessed. There, too, was the Princess's bed. Empty and lonely in the moonlight.

So much for the illness. Carefully, Lawler crawled back to the skylight and eased himself on to the step-ladder. Back into the living darkness of the stairs.

Now he had to reach Blackstone who would probably be in the Brown Bear. He returned to the servants' quarters feeling the miniature in his pocket. He felt as if it were glowing.

He went to his room and took his coat, pausing to load a pocket-pistol.

He let himself out into the courtyard and into the arms of Page.

'Hallo, Lawler,' Page said. 'Your night off, is it?'

'What do you want?'

'Just a few words.'

'I haven't time,' Lawler said, backing away.

'What's the matter? You needn't be afraid of me. . . .'

'Not now,' Lawler said.

'Yes, now, Lawler.'

'Sorry,' Lawler said. 'Some other time, my covey.'

He turned and ran, waiting again for the shot. But nothing happened. When he reached the road Page was still standing at the door, a haunted figure in the moonlight.

Chapter Four

····◊····

THE village lay about twenty miles outside London on the
way to Oxford. A few cottages, a small grey church kneeling
in the centre, two public houses, a coaching inn, a couple of
shops with merchandise faded by the departed summer and an
over-populated graveyard.

A mail coach was just departing from the inn – the village
stood at an important cross-roads – and vendors were trying
to make last sales to the occupants. Oranges, mostly, to remind
those bound for the far north of tropical London. They also
sold sponges, notebooks, handkerchiefs, sweetmeats, smelling
salts. . . .

From inside the coach four passengers looked down upon
them with tolerance. Another passenger sat beside the driver,
four more in a seat behind. At the back sat a guard with a
blunderbuss.

The driver cracked his whip and they were off, one vendor
being knocked off his feet by the barging flanks of the four
horses.

The courtyard was deflated after their departure. The men
counted their takings and headed for the pubs; the women
went home, except the bolder ones who agreed that a little
hot gin was the answer to the snapping afternoon. The boys
fought on the cobblestones and tried to sell the last few
oranges to Blackstone as he trotted into the courtyard on his
borrowed horse.

Inside, he sat down and ordered a hot whisky. He looked

at his watch. It was early afternoon; time was running out. But Challoner was nearby: he could feel it.

A fire blazed in the roomy grate and two old men sat in the inglenook toasting their faces. Behind Blackstone some country gentlemen were getting drunk and boasting that if Peel managed to get his bill banning man-traps and spring-guns passed they would ignore it. They were dressed in riding clothes, their beautiful tall hats hanging in a row in the hallway like fairground targets.

Other customers regarded them with hostility. The atmosphere was hot and rich; outside Blackstone noticed a group of labourers with leather-clothed legs, smock-frocks and iron beneath the soles of their shoes; they looked cold and poor.

Blackstone took some snuff. From the walls foxes snarled and glared at him with glassy ferocity. The gentlemen were having some sport with the serving girl; a little slapping and pinching which she accepted because it was their custom. She smiled at Blackstone.

One of the men asked Blackstone to have a drink. Blackstone accepted and ordered another hot whisky. Outside, the labourers, seven or eight of them, were having some sort of meeting.

The man who had offered Blackstone a drink said his name was John Saunders. 'Where are you from?' he asked. 'Your clothes have a city cut to them.'

'Paddington,' Blackstone told him.

'Ah.' Saunders looked disappointed.

'But I have my clothes made in St James's.'

Saunders brightened. 'What brings you to this part of the country?'

'Business,' Blackstone told him. He added: 'I deal in fire-arms.'

'Do you now.' Saunders told his three friends. 'Perhaps we could use some advice from you. We're having a little sport this afternoon.'

'Hunting?'

'In a way,' Saunders said. He was a big man, about twenty-five, too beefy for elegance. His hair was dark and thin, and there was a lot of down high on his cheeks. 'To tell you the truth,' he confided, 'we're not as drunk as we look.'

Blackstone said he was glad to hear it.

'Not by a long chalk,' Saunders said. He leaned forward. 'Can you keep a secret?'

'A gentleman can always keep a secret,' Blackstone said.

Saunders turned to his friends. 'Shall I tell him?'

'Why?' asked a middle-aged man called Willis who looked as if he might suffer from gout.

'He seems a decent sort. I thought he might like to join us. We might need some help with our guns.'

'What are you?' Willis asked. 'A gunsmith?'

'I buy and sell guns. I also collect them.'

'You have a strange accent,' Willis said. 'Not quite the thing somehow. I can't quite put my finger on it.'

'Really?' Blackstone controlled himself. 'A London accent perhaps instead of a country one.'

'All gentlemen speak the same,' Willis said.

Saunders said: 'Steady on.'

The girl came up with a tray of drinks and Blackstone thought briefly of the bed-warm body of the girl from the Brown Bear; and of Jane Hatherley.

'What's this sport you're having this afternoon?' he said.

Willis said: 'I want to know a little bit more about you. I want to know if you know anything about guns – not just how to make them.' He went outside and came back with a sporting gun. 'What can you tell me about that?'

Blackstone glanced at it. 'A fowling piece. About six years old but percussion lock. Octagonal 8-bore barrel at the breech, changing to circular. Made by Fuller of Wardour Street, I should think.' He leaned forward and moved Willis's index finger from the maker's name. 'Ah yes, Fuller. In this gun the fulminating powder is contained in copper tubes. One end of the tube faces the touch-hole. About fifty inches in length, I should think. Barrel length probably thirty-five inches.'

166

Saunders said: 'Is he right?' His cheeks were bright beneath the down.

Willis nodded. 'He's right enough. What do you think of the gun, Mr . . .'

'My name's Whitestone.' He took the gun from Willis. 'It's good enough for its purpose.'

'It cost enough,' Willis said.

'Let's not be sordid,' Blackstone said. 'Now tell me, what's the sport.'

'Saunders is quite right,' Willis said. 'It is a sort of a hunt.'

'A manhunt,' Saunders said.

Saunders, eager and flushed, explained that there had been a lot of trouble with poachers in the area. But they rarely got caught and he suspected they were working in league with the gamekeepers.

'How would that be?' Blackstone asked. 'What could they bribe the gamekeepers with?'

Saunders shrugged. 'Their sisters perhaps. You know what that class of people are like. And a cut of the money they get for whatever they bag. The gamekeepers aren't averse to a little extra on the side with no risk involved. Even though they're paid seventy guineas or so a year plus board and cottage. It's my belief they set the man-traps off before the poachers come into the woods.'

'And what,' Blackstone asked, 'is so special about this afternoon?'

Saunders said they had got wind of a big poaching foray. A military manœuvre almost. It was their intention to do battle with the poachers and to catch the gamekeepers collaborating.

'But they'll be armed,' Blackstone said. 'You stand as much chance of getting shot as they do.'

Saunders spread his hands, denoting bravery. 'It's about time someone taught them a lesson.'

Willis said: 'It's not quite such an equal battle as Saunders is making out.'

Saunders said: 'You can't expect us to commit suicide.'

'No,' Blackstone said, wondering why not.

In the first place, Willis explained, the poachers would be entering the forest expecting all the man-traps to have been rendered harmless. So, for that matter, would the gamekeepers. But the traps wouldn't be harmless. That was the first respect in which the odds were against the law-breakers. Secondly, the landowners intended to ambush them rather than conduct a more conventional military battle in which opposing armies face each other.

'How many of you will there be?' Blackstone asked.

'About twenty.'

'And how many poachers?'

'Seven or eight,' Willis said. He stretched his legs and Blackstone heard his knee click.

'Want to join us?' Saunders asked.

'It sounds like good sport,' Blackstone said. 'And you may need some help with your guns. I should have thought you would need some blunderbusses so that you can pepper them with lead.'

'We've got those,' Saunders assured him.

'And some trip wires,' Willis added.

'It'll certainly teach the bastards a lesson,' someone else said.

'Are you with us?' Saunders asked.

'Why not?' Blackstone said. 'But I've got some work to do first. I came here to buy some guns. Does a fellow called Charlston live up this way?'

They thought deeply, then shook their heads.

Blackstone said: 'Are you sure?'

'Wait a minute,' Saunders said. 'Didn't someone called Charlston rent The Grange about three months ago?'

'That's right,' Willis said. 'Rupert Charlston, wasn't it? But he's never lived in it as far as I know.'

'Where's The Grange?' The quarry strong in his nostrils once more.

'About two miles away. A nice old house lying off the road. But how can you be buying guns there if it's unoccupied?'

Saunders said: 'I'm not so sure that it is. I saw smoke

coming out of one of the chimneys this morning as I passed.'

'That would be it,' Blackstone said. 'I have an appointment there in half an hour.' He looked at his watch. 'I'd better be off.'

'Will you be joining us?' Saunders asked.

'I'll try. Where and what time?'

'Four o'clock. We're meeting at the big whitewashed barn on the edge of the woods on Willis's land. Not far from The Grange in fact.'

'I'll try and be there,' Blackstone said.

'Good man, Whitestone,' Saunders said.

The labourers had dispersed; the quarry, probably, for the manhunt.

Blackstone checked his guns. The holster pistols beside the saddle, and his two pocket pistols. In his boot was the French dirk.

He cantered for about a mile. Then took the horse into the woods beside the road and tethered it to a tree.

He walked on keeping just inside the woods, mostly beech, still brown and bronze in the afternoon sunshine. But already you could smell the evening cold arriving.

A wood pigeon fled from him, a red squirrel watched him; anticipation gathered tightly in his chest. He found he was holding his breath for no reason; he kicked a fungus from a tree trunk to relieve the tension.

The woods thinned after half a mile. His hands strayed to his guns. He became aware of this and was angry with himself.

The trees descended to bushes. Beyond lay a belt of grassland, then a high beech hedge. There was no cover between the woods and the hedge. Blackstone ran fast, keeping low, feeling his boots crunch on the frost crusting the grass.

He knelt behind the hedge, parting the dusty foliage and peering through. Ahead lay some stables, in the courtyard a blue and maroon carriage.

Somewhere beyond, Challoner. And the Princess.

And somewhere a look-out. Challoner might be confident he wouldn't be found, but he wouldn't be that careless.

Blackstone risked it again, from the hedge to the stables. He crouched behind the back wall, jumping as a horse inside kicked the woodwork. It whinnied and Blackstone pleaded with it to stop. Silence.

He peered round the wall. The house lay 150 yards away. A dignified, warm-bricked place with a terrace surrounded by stone flower-pots spaced at regular intervals. French-windows opened on to the terrace and there were steps leading on to a lawn that hadn't been mown for a long time. The lawn gave way to precise gardens patterned with miniature box hedges.

Blackstone searched for the look-out. The look-out obliged by rounding the terrace and posing at the top of the steps. A powerful, middle-aged man; but a little too relaxed for his duties.

Blackstone called on the horse to help him by knocking gently on the back of the stables. The horse kicked back. Blackstone knocked again and the horse whinnied.

The look-out stared in the direction of the stables.

Blackstone knocked once more and the horse responded with a lot more noise. The man came down the steps, not too urgently, and walked across the lawn towards the stables.

For a moment he was hidden by a summer house. Blackstone slipped inside the stable and waited beside the door. There were two horses inside. The one that had been making all the noise looked at him inquiringly; Blackstone put his finger to his lips but the horse took little notice.

'What's all the fuss?' the man said.

He pushed the door open and came in, pistol in hand. Blackstone chopped down with the blade of his right hand; the pistol fell into the hay.

Blackstone jabbed the pocket pistol into the man's ribs. 'Not a word,' he whispered. 'Not one whisper or you're a dead man. Now, hands up and turn around.'

'What the hell's going on?' the look-out said.

'What indeed.' Blackstone nudged his spine with the gun. 'Which room is she in?'

'Which room is who in? Are you a madman?'

Blackstone recognized the London voice. 'Which room has Challoner put her in?'

'I don't know what you're talking about.' He started to turn.

Blackstone said: 'Not another movement. This is a duelling pistol with a hair-trigger on it. Now, if you don't tell me which room these horses will be pulling your hearse.'

The man began to tremble. 'I don't know which room.'

'But you know what I'm talking about.'

'You mean the girl.'

'Yes,' Blackstone said. 'The girl.'

'I don't know. . . .'

'My name's Blackstone.'

'The Bow Street Runner?'

'The Bow Street Runner,' Blackstone said.

'I think it's on the second floor,' the look-out said. 'On the west wing. Where the chimney's smoking.'

'Whereabouts on the second floor.'

'I'm not sure. I think it's the second window along.'

'You'd better be right,' Blackstone said.

He clubbed the look-out behind the ear with the butt of the pistol. Then he gagged him, tied his wrists and ankles with some rope lying in the stable, and left him in the hay.

The stem of smoke was straight in the cooling sky. At its source was the Princess.

Blackstone ran to some trees at the side of the house where he paused. It was three o'clock. He wondered how Birnie had fared; how much time he had been given. He guessed that they had probably allowed him till ten; when they had digested their dinner, an hour or so before bed.

Seven hours to rescue the Princess and get her back to London. He took the dirk from his boot and slid the blade into the window of the pantry, searching for the catch.

Chapter Five

THERE wasn't much food in the pantry. A loaf of bread, a joint of beef, some pie, pickles, eggs, milk. Enough for, say, four for a couple of days. The Princess, the look-out, Challoner and one other. Probably a woman looking after the Princess.

But why? Blackstone asked himself again. If the motive was simply to clear the accession route to the throne why keep the Princess alive? Why hold her in a comfortable country house, keep her warm with a fire and apparently feed her well?

There was something inconsistent somewhere, a false note in the harmony of intrigue. Unless they did intend to kill her. Humane murderers who indulged their victims before executing them? Blackstone hadn't met their kind before.

He moved into the kitchen, gun in hand. It had a disturbed air about it; as if the presence of the former occupants had settled and then an intruder had arrived. The wooden table had been scrubbed recently, the plates on the shelves of the dresser were present-and-correct. Someone used to service was in charge of victualling.

On the wall beside the dresser was a glass case with bells inside. When the occupant of a room rang for service a tiny gong slipped down in front of the number of the room. Someone had rung from No. 14 and no one had bothered to slide the gong back. An imperious call from a princess?

Blackstone let himself out of the kitchen into a corridor. It smelled like a run-down hotel where no one exerts themselves until the wages are paid. An odour of stale food and unswept carpets.

He walked carefully, breathing the atmosphere. A sleeping place momentarily disturbed but not taking too much note. One day it might be aroused again by laughter and firelight; by gentlefolk and faithful retainers; but no temporaries would bother its repose.

The corridor led into a hall, minor baronial. There were a few pieces of furniture looking as if they had been delivered but not arranged. On the wall was an oil-painting of a big man in Jacobean dress with a face like a cocker spaniel amid long curls. Sir Joshua Charlston, Blackstone read. Surprising. He thought Charlston would have pawned all ancestral possessions: the frame would have fetched a few shillings.

He skirted the hall and reached the stairs. The house was thick with silence. No echoes, no clocks to give it the dimension of time.

He climbed the stairs gently. Not a creak. Sunlight examined the wainscoting, finding a few flaws. Blackstone reached the balcony overlooking the hallway. A grimy chandelier hanging over the hall tinkled beside him, its little frozen notes as sudden as gunfire in this absorbed place. Blackstone pressed himself against the wall in case the draught from an opening door had disturbed the chandelier. Nothing.

He prowled down the corridor leading to the right. It was covered with worn carpet. Rooms 1, 2, 3. . . . He took a bend and reached 9, 10, 11. Three more. He held the pistol lightly.

There was a large ornate key in the door of No. 14. He tried the handle first with butterfly touch, but it was locked. The key then. Please let it be oiled. He turned the key, the muscle in the ball of his thumb straining. It clicked softly, the sound as loud as a church bell in Blackstone's ears.

Now the handle again. The door opened six inches. He swept it open and went in, gun pointing.

The Princess turned, hand to her mouth. There was no one else in the room.

In one movement Blackstone crossed the room and clapped his hand round her mouth.

'Don't make a sound,' he whispered. 'Everything's going to be all right.'

He closed the door. It wasn't really the way to treat the heir to the throne, he thought.

Very quietly he explained to the Princess what they had to do. She listened carefully, nodding from time to time. Her composure, he thought, was extraordinary; formidable. He told her that they had to go downstairs, then they had to reach the woods beyond the grass. In the woods near the road he had a horse. They would ride back to the village on the horse where they would commandeer a carriage. They would be back in London by the late evening.

'I'm glad it was you, Blackstone,' she whispered.

'Who else?' He grinned at her.

What he didn't tell her was that first he had to get Challoner. The vague deceit worried him a little.

'You must wait just a little while in the stables,' he told her.

'Why?'

'Because,' he said.

He put her in an empty stable. She seemed to trust him and he felt guilty. But she was rescued and Challoner was still at large. It was his public duty to capture him. He remained unconvinced.

He closed the stable door and returned to the house. Through the pantry and kitchen and down the corridor to the hall. The Jacobean Charlston stared at him doggily.

Again the grimy chandelier made crystal music. He took no notice.

He pushed the half-open door of the dining-room. Had it been open before?

He was inside as Challoner spoke. 'Drop your pistol, Blackstone.'

Blackstone leaped back, firing as he went. The ball crashed through a window. Challoner's shot went through the chandelier, the remaining crystals playing a cracked jangling symphony.

Blackstone made the corridor as the second ball dug into the wainscoting. He crouched, waiting. He had one more barrel in one pistol; another two in the other. God knows what guns Challoner had.

He kept low, on his belly almost, and tried a shot round the corner. Challoner was across the hall by the portrait. They fired at the same time. Challoner's shot took a chunk off the corner above Blackstone's head; Blackstone's shot pierced the canvas heart of Sir Joshua Charlston; he looked as sad as ever.

Challoner shouted: 'You shouldn't have come, Blackstone. You're as good as dead.'

'Who put you up to this, Challoner?'

'Forget it.'

Blackstone backed down the passage because he was at a disadvantage there. A big target framed in a small aperture. As he reached the kitchen Challoner fired again, the ball punching a hole in the closing door.

Blackstone jumped out of the pantry window and ran round the house hoping to surprise Challoner from behind. He went in through the shattered dining-room window. The house was alive now with draughts and echoes. But Challoner had vanished.

He stalked Challoner. And knew that he himself was being stalked. Two men in a country house linked by a common denominator of ancestry.

He shouted to Challoner. His voice echoed and was lost in the astonished house.

Then he remembered the Princess. If Challoner had seen him take her to the stables. . . . He ran to the terrace and headed for the stables. The Princess was still there, sitting in the straw.

'Are you all right?'

She nodded.

'Stay there. Don't move.'

As he came out he saw Challoner duck behind one of the sentinel stone pots on the terrace.

There were two more shots. But not from Challoner. They sounded as if they were about a quarter of a mile away. He peered round the stables and saw men on the grass separating the beech hedge from the woods. The manhunt was on.

He shouted to Challoner. 'You might as well give up, Challoner. Here come the rest of the search party.'

Challoner fired back. No hope of hitting Blackstone, who was behind cover. Just defiance.

No movement now from behind the stone pot. Blackstone reloaded the two pistols. Still no movement. He fired, smashing the big ornate bowl. No Challoner.

Blackstone looked around. Challoner was half way across the grass heading for the woods.

Blackstone swore and ran after him. But Challoner had a hundred-yard start. He was in the woods by the time Blackstone was half way across the grass.

When Blackstone reached the trees there were more shots. And shouts and curses from both sides. Man-hunters and poachers were doing battle; and he was stalking Challoner in between them.

He lay quiet, smelling the earth. The beech leaves above were still bronze against the retiring sky, but the mists were rising and the green cushion of moss was set with diamonds of ice. There was a lull in the shooting: Blackstone listened for other movements. But Challoner was lying low. This was the way it always was: they had the same minds and the same tactics.

He watched a black beetle making its way through the green hills of moss. High above, the crows were settling again after the shooting. Behind, the windows of The Grange played with the sunlight. He could feel his heart against the moss.

A movement ahead.

A volley of shots from both sides. If he stayed he stood a good chance of being mown down by either side. He knew his duty was to the Princess waiting for him in the stable. He stayed.

The man-hunters were shouting a lot. The poachers remained

silent because they knew about this sort of game. Perhaps the ambush had failed. He hoped so.

He began to move forward on his belly to see if the volleys had hit anything. He reached the tree where he had noticed the movement. There was nothing there. Except a copper percussion cap glinting in the thin woodland grass. It was the sort Challoner would use: it was the type he used.

To his left the gentlemen were making a lot of noise breaking twigs, laughing uneasily. They should have had beaters, he thought.

To the right a scream of agony.

'That's got one of the bastards.' It sounded like Saunders's voice. 'He's walked straight into a man-trap. Now let them have it.'

Gun-fire exploded all around, the balls tearing through the branches and scattering the birds again. Another cry of pain from the poachers' ranks; another man-trap or a shot that had found a target.

Where the hell was Challoner?

The hunters were advancing. A couple of blunderbusses loosed off. The lead-shot made harmless sounds in the trees. But one small ball of lead buried itself in Blackstone's left shoulder. He felt the warm flow of blood down his arm.

He thought he saw Willis about fifty yards away behind a thicket. He took aim with his good arm, then lowered his pistol – that wasn't what this was all about.

His left arm was weakening, the cold spreading through his body. Cold everywhere except in the small wound itself. Blackstone thought it might have punctured a big vein. There was nothing he could do about it now.

To the right a single booming shot and more enthusiasm from the hunters. 'One of them's tripped off a spring-gun,' someone called.

'I don't think it hit him,' someone else shouted.

'Shame.' Saunders's voice.

The blood so warm, the limb so cold.

He had to get Challoner. Now. Before he passed out.

But where? It was as if Challoner knew he was wounded and was waiting for him to weaken. Like Cato Street.

From the poachers' end of the woods there was no movement. The gentlemen were still advancing. They reached Blackstone as he stood up, leaning against a tree for cover.

'Whitestone.' It was Saunders. 'What are you doing here, man?'

'I got lost. . . .'

'Never mind. I think we've just about finished them off. You can join us for the mopping-up operation.' He noticed the blood on Blackstone's limp arm. 'Are you hurt?'

Blackstone didn't bother to reply.

Saunders was carrying a fowling piece which he was reloading. They were joined by Willis who carried a blunderbuss and a couple of holster pistols in his belt.

Saunders said: 'Don't worry, Whitestone, we'll avenge you.'

'Except that it was your shot that hit me.'

Just ahead of them grew a thicket of holly. Behind it the outline of a crouching man.

Challoner sensed he had been spotted and began to run.

Blackstone tried to run after him but the cold had reached his feet and they were weighted with ice.

'There,' he shouted. 'There's a poacher getting away.' He turned to Saunders. 'Don't let him get away.'

'He won't get away,' Saunders said. He took aim and missed. 'Don't worry, I'll get the bastard.' He ran after Challoner.

Willis tried to stop him and someone else called after him: 'Don't be a fool, Saunders.'

But the scent of poacher's blood was in Saunders's nostrils.

The figure of Challoner vanished behind the bole of a beech tree. Then reappeared twenty-five yards further on veering from side to side.

He was gaining on Saunders and Saunders realized it. He was slowing down, accepting defeat, when the jaws of the mantrap, concealed in a shallow pit and covered with branches and leaves, snapped at him, severing his foot just above the ankle.

The doctor dressed the small wound on his shoulder and said: 'You were lucky.'

'Is it lucky to be shot, doctor?'

'Luckier than Saunders.'

'Yes,' Blackstone said, 'luckier than Saunders.'

He sat on a faded sofa in the hall strewn with glass tears from the chandelier. The wound was plugged and he had found some brandy. He felt stronger but the knowledge of Challoner's escape made his thoughts stride around restlessly. The emotion was stronger than relief at rescuing the Princess, now waiting for him in the room where she had been held prisoner. But what was the emotion? Disappointment, certainly. Failure. But somewhere amid it all a gleam of relief. He remembered the shots they had taken at each other; missing all the time, as if some unrealized compulsion was making each of them aim fractionally off target. No, surely not. He had been aiming to kill: his finger tightened round a phantom trigger as he saw Challoner again in the hallway. But did the sights waver? Blackstone shook his head. He would hunt Challoner down in London and when he caught him. . . .

The doctor said: 'Apparently Saunders and his bunch weren't as clever as they thought. The poachers knew they planned a battle this afternoon and they moved all the mantraps. The gamekeepers must have had something to do with it. You should never antagonize your gamekeeper.'

Blackstone said: 'It sounded as if the gamekeepers had casualties.'

The doctor shook his head. 'Not as far as we can make out. They must have been pretending to encourage the *enemy* to come forward. Another of the landowners got a blast from a spring-gun.' He rolled down his sleeves and pointed at Sir Joshua's wound. 'What happened here?'

'A chance shot from the battle,' Blackstone told him.

'And what do you propose to do now?'

'I have to ride back to London.'

'You'll be very foolish if you try.'

'I have to,' Blackstone said. He looked at his watch. 'Now.'

'You won't make it. Not in your condition. You've lost a fair amount of blood.'

'I have to make it,' Blackstone said. He stood up. A little dizziness at first, but it soon passed. 'Thank you, doctor.' He gave him some money.

'Why is it so important?'

'Business,' Blackstone said. 'Unfinished business.'

The doctor shrugged. 'I can only advise you.'

'I'm obliged.'

Blackstone waited for him to leave.

He checked the house to see if there was any sign of the woman who had been guarding the Princess. But she had fled. He went to the stable and cut the ropes from the lookout's hands; he would be able to free himself within a few minutes.

The Princess seemed excited, nothing more.

Together they skirted the battlefield, heading for the tethered horse. Night was crowding around them. Frost crisping, mist settling, the sun bloody to the west.

'We'll have to ride fast,' he said.

'I feel quite safe with you, Blackstone,' she told him.

He considered the possibility that Challoner was lying in wait for him; then rejected it. Challoner would presume that the whole area was on the alert for him now. He would be escaping; galloping, perhaps, on a stolen horse towards the anonymity of London.

He found the horse and put the Princess in front of him. As he urged the horse through the fleeting countryside he knew that there was still an inconsistency lodged like a foreign body in the fabric of the affair. He would have to find it and remove it.

Chapter Six

·····⚜·····

It was 9.15pm. In London several eminent men watched the evening shrinking on their clocks with apprehension.

The Prime Minister, the second Earl of Liverpool, sat in his study in the old home of Sir Robert Walpole at No. 10 Downing Street watching the spidery finger of an old grandfather clock with feelings close to physical illness.

He was old and he had ruled – or tried to rule as much as two Georges had allowed him – for a long time. Fourteen years, wasn't it? Ambition, never extravagant, had spent its course leaving him with an autumnal desire to be remembered affectionately as a Tory Prime Minister who had made room for stability after Waterloo. History would not allow him much space; he knew that. Solid. He could see the students rustling quickly through *his* pages in search of the era's luminaries. Peel, Canning, Huskisson. Liverpool harboured no jealousy: they had shone under his mantle of stability.

All he desired now was a gentle climax devoid of public outrage, war or scandal.

The Prime Minister Who Delayed Announcing the Abduction of Princess Alexandrina Victoria With Tragic Consequences.

The minute hand of the clock stabbed forward and he felt a tiny pain in his chest. He should never have agreed to this delay. His country might be on the verge of terrible instability that would continue far beyond his span. The historians would make great play of that.

9.18. Stability spiked on the jerky finger of the old clock. My life, he thought, is on the tip of that finger.

Nearby, in an office in Whitehall, Robert Peel envisaged the chaos that would follow a public announcement of the Princess's abduction and planned how to contain it. At the very least there would be action against Cumberland whom the British people detested. The anger might extend to the whole Court of St James's if the beliefs of the Duchess of Kent and Sir John Conroy that George had connived at the abduction became public knowledge. Peel planned control of initial outrage, then disobedience on the scale of the Gordon Riots, then civil war. He allowed for all eventualities, and considered each with controlled sorrow. He also discussed with himself the delegation of responsibility for the abduction. It would be cowardly to try and lay the whole responsibility with the Bow Street Runners. The overall responsibility was his. But the role of the Runners was certainly inglorious and he wouldn't hesitate to emphasize this in debate. If an adequate police force had been in existence, Peel mused, the kidnapping wouldn't have happened. Perhaps now his uniformed dreams of law and order would be realized sooner than he expected. He glanced at his watch. 9.20. They would have the public announcement for the newspapers prepared by midnight. Then the news would be released by messengers, mail coach, pigeons, and boat, all over Britain and the rest of the world. Provided, of course, that Edmund Blackstone didn't manage to rescue the Princess. Peel thought this unlikely.

Lawler took a hackney carriage from Kensington to Bow Street, determining, as it passed through the West End, to add the fare to his payment. In the carriage he was no longer a footman. He was happy to have this rest from acting; although he wasn't always sure when he was on or off stage. The facts which he had to convey to Blackstone were carefully packaged in his mind. The alleged illness of the Princess, her absence and the finding of the miniature. He felt important with all this information; but a sense of grievance also lingered because he was anticipating the smallness of the reward for his initiative – in fact, there might not be a reward at all. He would only do this for Blackstone. No one else. But if Blackstone wasn't there, what should he do? He supposed he would have to see the beak – the old man Birnie. Lawler didn't fancy that. He wished, as he had wished before, that he had never struck a bet with Blackstone all those years ago. Or did he?

In the Palace of ticking clocks the Duchess of Kent stared at her daughter's empty bed and wept. In a room close by Fräulein Lehzen paused in the midst of her weeping to pop some caraway seed in her mouth, then wept on. In the servants' quarters a nursemaid, a lady's-maid and a housemaid planned marital bliss with the new footman in various suburbs of London.

In his office overlooking the Brown Bear, Sir Richard Birnie poked the fire with finality and made a full confession to himself. A vainglorious life full of arid ambition was ending in ignominy. He gestured hopelessly to Henry Fielding, to John Fielding, to Saunders Welch: the ancestry he had betrayed. Within an hour a decision would be taken that would make the failure of the Bow Street Runners public knowledge. He heard the wind on the moors, smelled the heather and felt smooth hides in his saddlemaker's hands. Too late. A lifetime too late. He wondered what had happened to Blackstone; but only vaguely. The hope that had made him plead for a day's grace had faded. He regretted Blackstone's suspension; his own action seemed at this desolate time to have a ring of treachery about it.

He stirred the thick ash with the poker.

And would Blackstone, with whom he had an affinity, for whom he felt responsibility, return to crime?

Best, perhaps, that he did.

The old man – older today than ever before – took his coat and his hat and his cane.

He was about to leave when Lawler was ushered in by the duty officer.

Lawler said: 'I want to see Mr Blackstone.'

'Who are you?' Birnie asked.

'It doesn't matter who I am. I've got some information for him.'

Birnie looked at him without interest. An informer. A criminal who betrayed criminals. The lowest species. A class of men indispensable to crime prevention and detection, a class whose value Birnie acknowledged – and eschewed.

'What information?' Birnie asked.

'It's for Mr Blackstone's ears only.'

'I don't know where Blackstone is. What's more I've no time to waste.'

Lawler wasn't sure whether it was in Blackstone's interests to confide in the old man. But it was Blackstone's initiative that had enabled him, Lawler, to discover that the Princess was apparently missing.

He said: 'I've been working for Mr Blackstone at Kensington Palace. I believe Princess Drina may have come to some harm.' It sounded very formal.

Birnie nodded. 'Really?'

The sense of grievance returned. As if Birnie were trying to minimize the importance of his information – and minimize any reward. 'Did you know about it?' he asked belligerently. He wasn't a defendant, he didn't have to crawl.

'It doesn't matter. I'm obliged for your help. Now I have to go.'

'Hey,' Lawler said, 'just a minute.'

Birnie looked at him with distaste. 'You'll get your money,' he said.

'I wasn't thinking about that,' Lawler lied. He put his hand in his pocket. 'Don't tell me you knew about this.' He handed Birnie the miniature.

'What's this?'

Lawler told him.

'That's interesting,' Birnie said, addressing Henry Fielding and his blind half-brother. 'At least we've salvaged something.'

Lawler said: 'I beg your pardon?' He was beginning to doubt Birnie's sanity.

'At least the Bow Street Runners found the child's miniature.' He headed for the door.

'I'm going to wait here until Mr Blackstone returns,' Lawler
told him.

'Please yourself,' Birnie said. 'But please wait downstairs.'

Lawler held out his hand. 'The miniature, sir. Could I have
it back please?'

Birnie gave it back to him. They walked down the stairs
together.

Lawler decided to wait for Blackstone in the Brown Bear.
Birnie took a hackney carriage to Downing Street.

Chapter Seven

···✠···

WITH nightfall came a thaw, and rain. The rain started like heavy mist, then thickened, taking on a slant in the light of the carriage lamps. Inside the carriage sat the Princess, outside sat Blackstone urging on the horses, inadequate clothes pasted to his body by the rain. He felt vulnerable up there with the wet night streaming past him, and he thought the Princess accepted her snug role with divine right. The wound was aching, the arm felt boneless.

As he drove, calling on the horses rather than whipping them, he wondered about the inconsistency in the pattern. It was a simple inconsistency: you don't kidnap a Princess without a reason. And unless Challoner had planned to murder her – intuitively Blackstone doubted this – there was no apparent reason. But, of course, there was.

He surged past a mail coach pulling out from an inn. The lights from the inn lit pools of water in the mud on the road. The heads and manes of the horses became part of the night.

He arrived at Kensington Palace at 9.30. He drove up to the doors in wild style, told the Princess to wait in the carriage and rang the bell. A footman – not Lawler – answered. Blackstone pushed him aside and went inside. 'Fetch Sir John Conroy,' he told the protesting footman.

The footman began to speak but Blackstone interrupted him. 'Just get him.' He waited, feeling the water running down his body and collecting in his boots. Steam was probably rising from him. He began to shiver. He noticed the water dripping on to the floor was tinged with blood.

Conroy was wearing a plum-coloured smoking jacket and his breath smelled faintly of brandy. 'Blackstone,' he said. 'What the hell are you doing here?' He took in Blackstone's appearance. 'Good God, what's happened?'

Blackstone said: 'Get rid of him.' He pointed at the hovering footman.

Conroy did so without enthusiasm. 'Now, just what do you think you're doing?'

Blackstone said: 'I've found the Princess.'

'You've what?'

'She's outside.'

Conroy looked stunned. Then he said: 'Bring her in for God's sake! Is she all right? Is she well?'

'She's all right. I don't want anyone to see her yet. I want you to get her up to her room. Keep her there till I come back. Don't let her talk to any servants. Just her mother and Fräulein Lehzen.'

'Tell me,' Conroy said, 'what happened?'

'Later. I have to see Birnie before the Prime Minister and Peel decide to tell the world.'

He took Conroy by the arm and led him out into the rain which ravaged his velvet jacket.

Blackstone stole a horse from the stables and set out on the last stretch. He wouldn't be able to make it much farther. Once he seemed momentarily to lose consciousness. Perhaps not. All sensation was coalescing. He had to stop them. Had to stop them. Stop them.

But Birnie wasn't at Bow Street.

He crossed the road with a drunken waltzing walk and went into the Brown Bear. One or two Runners were sitting at a table. They called out to him in astonishment.

The girl came up. 'Blackie,' she said. 'Blackie.'

He nodded.

'Where's Birnie?' he asked.

'We don't know,' they said.

187

'You must know.'

The girl said: 'Sit down, Blackie. Please sit down and I'll get you a hot whisky.'

He tried to smile at her but his face was frozen. 'Bring the whisky,' he told her.

'What's happened?' It was Ruthven.

'It doesn't matter. I have to find Birnie.'

Lawler tapped him on the shoulder. 'I think I know where he is.'

Blackstone turned. 'What the hell are you doing here?'

'I've got to speak to you.'

'Not now. Not now.' He poured the hot whisky down his throat; it dropped into his stomach like molten metal.

Lawler touched his arm again, the bad one. 'It's important.'

Blackstone realized what he had said. 'You know where Birnie is?'

Lawler nodded. The ingratitude was beginning to sicken him.

'Where?'

'Downing Street,' Lawler said. 'I heard him tell the driver.'

'Come on.'

No one said anything very much. They all stared at him. The girl began to speak but Blackstone put his finger to his lips.

He went outside with Lawler and asked him to fetch a cab. What else was it that Lawler had to tell him? he asked when the cab arrived.

Lawler told him the Princess was missing. Blackstone began to laugh. The laughter had an hysterical note to it.

'What's so funny?' Lawler asked when they were seated. He added: 'I'll tell you what, Blackie, I'm through with this. You can blackmail me as much as you like, throw me into Newgate, put me on the hulks, transport me – I'm not doing any more jobs for you. Christ,' he went on, 'do you realize what I said? Princess Drina's missing. Poor little bitch,' he added.

'I'm sorry,' Blackstone said.

'You're what?' Lawler asked in disbelief.

Blackstone sank into the corner and closed his eyes. The darkness pulsed around him. He was aware of his pulse beat, as slow as the waves. No, he thought, I mustn't close my eyes. Otherwise I shan't open them again tonight and Birnie will have lost. We will have lost. The Bow Street Runners. He put his hand to the pocket of his greatcoat heavy with water. The baton was there. He levered his eyelids open. 'What else, Lawler?' he asked. 'What else?'

'What else do you want?'

'Anything, Lawler. Anything. Do you have anything more to tell me?'

Lawler handed him the miniature. 'I thought you might be interested in this.' He was gratified by Blackstone's reaction.

The cab was heading down Whitehall.

Blackstone said: 'Amy Hucklestone, eh?'

Lawler nodded. 'A good little moll.'

'Yes,' Blackstone agreed, 'a good girl.'

'We don't have to arrest her, do we, Mr Blackstone?'

'I don't know,' Blackstone said. 'I don't know.' He tried to sit upright but it was an effort. Not long now. He wouldn't be able to remain upright or conscious much longer. The blood was freezing, the rain outside was floating like snow. To keep his lips and tongue working he asked: 'Anything more, Lawler?'

'Christ,' Lawler said. 'What do you want – blood?'

'Yes,' Blackstone said.

'Nothing more. Except a lot of gossip about Conroy flirting with the Princess's mother and that other woman, Princess Sophie of somewhere or other.'

'Oh yes,' Blackstone said.

He wasn't allowed into the sanctum where they were discussing the emergency. He hadn't expected to be. He waited inside the door while a suspicious footman took a message to Birnie after posting another suspicious footman to keep an eye on him.

Blackstone thought Birnie looked about ninety. But who was he to pass judgement on appearance? He told Birnie that the emergency was over: that the Bow Street Runners had found the missing Princess. Vindication. He attempted a ghastly smile.

Birnie didn't seem to know what to do. He tried to shake Blackstone's bad arm; then he raised his hands in delayed surprise. Finally he said: 'Thank you, Blackie.' A touch of moorland health already regrouping in his cheeks.

So what did you say? Think nothing of it, sir?

Blackstone fainted.

Much later, after medical attention and congratulation, after hearing that he had saved England, after promises of financial reward, after the whole performance, Blackstone said he was well enough to leave.

Birnie shook his good arm. 'You've done well, Blackie,' he reiterated. They stood on the doorstep.

'Thank you, sir.' Blackstone's hand went to the new bandage the doctor had just put round his shoulder. 'What about my job?'

Birnie said: 'I know you feel bitter, Blackstone. But it was for the best. The Bow Street Runners come first. You know that.'

'Yes,' Blackstone said. 'I know that. But what about my job? What about the threat to publish the details of my brutal behaviour if I'm not dismissed?'

'Forget all about it,' Birnie said. 'You're a hero.'

'Hardly,' Blackstone said. 'I can't be a hero for rescuing a Princess when it's been agreed that no one shall ever know she was missing.'

'Peel knows,' Birnie said smugly.

'Ah, Peel.'

'And the Prime Minister.' As if he were less important. 'The reputation of the Bow Street Runners is assured.'

Blackstone said: 'And Lawler did find the missing miniature.'

'Yes,' Birnie said. 'I'd almost forgotten that.' He thought about it. 'That does make you a hero.' Ignoring the part played by Lawler. 'Everyone can know about that. Beating a groom? It hardly matters any more. Peel will have to acknowledge the part played by the Bow Street Runners.'

It sounded more important than the rescue of the Princess. Blackstone said: 'I'm glad about that, sir.'

'Good.' Birnie put his arm round Blackstone's shoulders. 'Now you'd better be on your way. Straight back to bed, mind. Let me know when you're feeling better.'

'I will,' Blackstone said.

He remembered that Lawler was still waiting in the cab outside. 'Give my regards to the Prime Minister. Tell him I'm sorry I bled on his carpet.'

Birnie didn't laugh.

Outside, Blackstone asked the driver to take Lawler and himself to Kensington Palace.

The dreams had a lurching quality about them that awoke him many times during the night. Rain in his face, tossing manes, guns exploding in his hand. But towards dawn they calmed down; and his waking moments were lucid, as if he were peering through deep clear water. Minor experiences, irrelevant during the galloping day, were still lodged in his mind, pressing for explanation. He reached the conversation with Lawler outside the Brown Bear. Then he realized that there was only one person who could benefit by the kidnapping. Could still benefit. The moment was very lucid, the water very deep.

The woman in the bed beside him kissed him gently. 'Go back to sleep,' she said.

'Jane Hatherley,' he said.

'Hallo, Blackie,' she said.

He returned to sleep and stayed there peacefully for several hours.

Chapter Eight

⋯⋯⋯⋯

SIR JOHN CONROY gestured to the chair in front of his mahogany desk with its green, gold-embossed leather top and said: 'Sit down, Blackstone.'

Blackstone sat down.

'A drink?'

'No thanks.' He took some snuff from the Nathaniel Mills box that had stayed with him throughout yesterday.

'You've done well, Blackstone. Very well. I shouldn't be surprised if there isn't a substantial reward in it for you.'

'That would be acceptable,' Blackstone told him.

'The great pity is that you'll never receive the recognition you deserve. I was in touch with Downing Street this morning and the decision is that this whole affair must be kept secret. Not too many people know about it. You and me, Birnie, the Duchess and Fräulein Lehzen, the criminals involved, the Prime Minister and one or two ministers. Each of us can be relied on to keep quiet. We all have good reason to. The German ladies for the safety of the Princess – this sort of thing being infectious if it's publicized. The criminals because they certainly won't want to invite arrest. The Ministers for the sake of British prestige – and their own reputations. I know you and Birnie can be trusted.'

'Yes,' Blackstone said. 'We can be trusted.' He toyed with the warm silver snuff-box. 'And you, Conroy, can you be trusted?'

'I hardly think I need answer that.' His finger sawed at the cleft in his chin. 'You know about the promises I made the Princess's father. Her safety means everything to me.'

'I believe that,' Blackstone said. 'Otherwise you wouldn't have had the fire lit in her room in The Grange. And you wouldn't have bothered to see she was well fed.'

Conroy drummed his thick fingers on the desk. 'What are you talking about, Blackstone?'

'You know what I'm talking about. You looked pretty scared last night when I said I'd found the Princess.'

'Scared? Astonished. Delighted.' He clasped his hands and leaned forward. 'Are you feeling quite yourself, Blackstone? You should have stayed in bed for a few days.' He managed to smile, man-to-man. 'With someone to keep you warm.'

'You were astonished all right. And scared. I suppose you thought you were quite safe with Challoner working for you and Charlston out of the way.'

'I think we'd better talk another time. When you're feeling better.'

'No,' Blackstone said, 'we'll talk now.'

Conroy said: 'I'm going to ring for a servant to see you out.'

'Please do.'

Conroy didn't move. 'It might be amusing to hear the rest of your theory,' he said.

'Very well. It was Lawler who put me on to you. He told me about your flirtations with the Duchess of Kent.'

'That's a highly slanderous statement.'

'Sue me,' Blackstone said.

'Perhaps I will. Please continue.'

'I realized for the first time how desperate you are to assure yourself of the good life in the future. To do this you have to be in favour with the women of this German household. In particular the Duchess. Equally you have to foster ill-feeling between Kensington Palace and the Court of St James so that you'll be preferred when your little Drina becomes Queen. You wouldn't stand much chance with some of the competition around at St James's Palace, Conroy.'

'Thank you,' Conroy said.

'So you started the rumours about the Princess's life being

in danger and got the Duchess worrying – not a difficult task. You also pointed the finger at Cumberland and got the Duchess in such a state that she even thought the King was in the plot to let Uncle Ernest accede to the throne. All that worked, of course. Hostility between the two factions has never been worse. Fine. Your standing in the Kensington fortress couldn't have been better: your future in the Queen's court seemed assured.'

'I trust it still is,' Conroy said, smiling and tapping away with his fingers. It could have been the National Anthem that he was drumming.

'But you're an ambitious man, Conroy. And your plans had to be ambitious. So you decided to fake an abduction that would turn the whole of the country against the Court of St James.'

'Even more so than they are now?'

Blackstone nodded. 'Even more so. You would have emerged as the man who warned the Duchess. And I suspect you would also have emerged as the man who rescued her. That wouldn't have been difficult, would it, Conroy? As you were the only man who knew where she was, apart from Challoner and his accomplices.'

Blackstone walked to the window. It was a gusty, kite-flying day.

'I think perhaps I will have a drink,' Conroy said. 'You?'

'All right,' Blackstone said.

'Hot rum?'

Blackstone nodded.

'I hope it doesn't inflame your imagination any more.'

'But, of course, you had to arrange protection for the Princess because of the rumours you had started about her safety.' Blackstone went on after the maid had brought the drinks. 'Enter the Bow Street Runners.' He paused. 'The next part is guesswork.'

'The rest isn't, of course.'

'I think Challoner wanted me out of the way. I knew his style. Also there is personal rivalry between us. . . . And perhaps you both thought I might be getting too close to the truth about Charlston, your accomplice.'

'Poor Charlston,' Conroy said.

'I presume Challoner arranged about the incident with the groom. Sworn statements from a few criminals, the assistance of a crooked lawyer and there I was. Fixed.' He took some snuff reflectively. 'Your next target was Charlston. After he had tried to kill me with the assistance of Jane Hatherley. Did you know about that, Conroy? I suppose it would have suited your book if we had killed each other.'

'You don't imagine I'm going to answer such a question?'

'Not really.' Blackstone sipped his rum. His arm was beginning to hurt again and he was tiring. 'Maybe Charlston just wanted me out of the way because I was blackmailing him into helping me. But you certainly wanted him out of the way, didn't you, Conroy? He was your accomplice, he was the one who rented The Grange where the Princess was to be hidden. He was the only man apart from Challoner who knew the truth. Was he blackmailing you, Conroy?'

Conroy took a quick swig of rum; he didn't reply.

Blackstone said: 'So you hired a professional killer to get him involved in a duel. Charlston never stood a chance. Then the kidnap, and the emergence of Sir John Conroy as saviour and hero. But it's not going to be like that, is it, Conroy?'

'It certainly isn't going to be like that,' Conroy said. 'It never was. What's more you can never prove it. The Duchess of Kent trusts me implicitly. You say Charlston hired this house. He's dead. This man Challoner – he certainly won't come forward. You can convey your theory to anyone you like, Blackstone. I may sue you, I may not.'

'I don't think you will.' The ache in his arm was a throb: rum didn't seem to be a pain-killer. 'I shall certainly convey my theory,' Blackstone said. 'I agree that I can't prove much of it. But I feel that history will judge you, Conroy. I'm sure of one thing – you'll go on scheming. You haven't finished with Cumberland yet. And I'm damned sure you haven't finished with the Duchess – or the Princess Sophie,' he added.

'You'll go on scheming, but I shall let a lot of people who matter know about you. I don't think you'll be taken too seriously again. And you like to be taken seriously, don't you, Conroy?'

Conroy shrugged. 'I could get your reward increased . . .'

'Forget it.'

Perhaps, Blackstone thought, a word in the Princess's ear. He finished his rum and walked into the corridor.

Lawler was downstairs. And Page.

Page said: 'Congratulations, Blackie.'

'Thank you.'

'No hard feelings?' His hands fluttered anxiously from pocket to pocket.

There were hard feelings, of course. 'No,' Blackstone said, grinning. 'Just stick to pickpockets.'

Lawler said: 'A word in your ear, Blackie.' He drew him to one side and whispered: 'What shall I do with the miniature?'

'Give it back, of course. You weren't thinking of pinching it, were you?'

'No,' Lawler said without conviction. 'But what about the girl?'

'Say you found it in the garden. Say anything you like. Say you found it among Fräulein Lehzen's caraway seeds.' He looked at Lawler speculatively. 'Thinking of settling down, Lawler?'

'I don't know,' Lawler said. 'What sort of reward do you think I'll get?'

'Enough to settle down with.'

'That's what I was afraid of,' Lawler said. 'Good-bye, Blackie.' He almost ran towards the main door. 'I'm glad it worked out all right. . . .'

Blackstone nodded, his mind elsewhere. Lawler thought Blackstone might have thanked him.

There were three of them in the room – the Duchess, Fräulein

Lehzen and the Princess. He wished the two German women were elsewhere: he didn't enjoy hysterical gratitude. They clasped their hands and tearfully said they didn't know how to thank him. He told them in cash terms. The Princess sat in a nursery chair, promoting it to a throne. Blackstone smiled at her. 'I hope they've told you you must never mention a word of this, Your Highness. Not in your future journals, not in your lifetime.'

'Yes, Blackstone,' she said. 'They've told me.' She paused. 'We understand.' She gave him her little paw.

That left Jane Hatherley. They stood facing each other outside the Palace, a wind tugging at her dress. Her face was very pale, her hair very bright. 'That day beside the river,' she said, 'I did try to save you.'

'I know,' he said.

'But you're going, aren't you?'

A glint of river like a fish leaping, the chestnut smell of fallen leaves, a kiss.

He nodded. 'We have to keep to our own kind.'

'Why, Blackie? Why?' She was crying.

'Because,' he said.

He took a hackney carriage and told the driver to take him to the Brown Bear where the girl would be waiting for him. In the carriage he fancied he could hear clocks ticking all around him. The sensation lasted a moment; then it was behind him.

THE END

Epilogue

••◦••

THE alleged Cumberland Plot continued to burgeon, reaching the height of its notoriety a few years later. Rumours concerning the safety of Princess Alexandrina Victoria were disseminated in 'informed circles' while gossip about an affair between Sir John Conroy and the Duchess of Kent became common in society circles. The Conroy camp blamed Cumberland for the latter claiming that he wanted the King to remove the Princess from such an atmosphere of immorality. In the end no one benefited from allegation, rumour or gossip. When Queen Victoria acceded to the throne Cumberland left to be King of Hanover; and on the first day of her reign she banished Conroy from her Household. And many years later she ridiculed any suggestion of a Cumberland Plot.

HISTORICAL NOTE

The Bow Street Runners

THE Bow Street Runners were the forerunners of the Metropolitan Police established by Sir Robert Peel in 1829. The first reference to the Runners appeared in the *Morning Herald* in 1785. But they had existed long before without such grand designation. Their inception was probably in 1749 when the Bow Street Magistrate, Henry Fielding, author of *Tom Jones*, enrolled six volunteer thief-takers. Such was the secrecy of their methods, and such was public hostility to thief-takers (Jonathan Wild, the original of Peachum in *The Beggar's Opera*, being the most notorious), that there is not much documentation about their beginnings. By 1797 this embryonic Flying Squad of six or eight operators was firmly established and by 1821 had reached the height of its swaggering fame.

Every police force is vulnerable to accusations of corruption: certainly the Bow Street Runners were no exception: indeed perhaps more vulnerable because, like today's private eyes, they often acted for private individuals or corporations and were accused of acting as intermediaries between thief and victim, i.e. returning stolen property to the owner and extracting both a reward and a promise that he would not prosecute.

The Runners survived for ten years after the formation of the Metropolitan Police, but the relationship between the two was bitter. The Runners' chief, the Bow Street Magistrate Richard Birnie, said of the new police with their chimney-pot hats: 'I never saw a constable who was perfectly competent'. But the new 'Peelers' or 'Bobbies' won in the end and in 1839 the Bow Street Runners were disbanded; although some continued their private police work which took them on many a desperate pursuit across Europe and America.

During their ninety years' existence they policed London when it was a mattress for the bed-bugs of every crime and vice; every facet of poverty, every indulgence of luxury. Highwaymen, child prostitutes and child debauchers, smugglers, street thugs, animal-baiters, thieves and crooked thief-takers; gin shops, stinking boarding-houses crammed with the poor, pawnshops, poor houses and debtors' jails. Name the crime, name the depravity, name the deprivation: London had it.

Execution was a popular spectacle and it was not until 1817 that the public flogging of girl offenders, stripped to the waist, was abolished. In 1819 there were 223 offences punishable by death and it was possible to be hanged for impersonating a Chelsea Pensioner or chipping pieces off Westminster Bridge.

That was the Bow Street Runners' scene, and during their reign they laid the groundwork for today's methods of criminal detection: fraternization with villains (as dubious in the eyes of the Establishment then as it is now), exhaustive inquiries, hunting for clues, even rudimentary ballistics. Also they attended riots and massacres spawned by the working classes' unforgivable aspirations to be treated like human beings which make present-day London – perhaps Washington and New York even – seem like sanctuaries.

During this period there were other police units such as the uniformed horse patrols, responsible for dispersing the highwaymen, and foot patrols which, in 1822, were given a uniform complete with a red waistcoat by Peel. Both are sometimes confused with the Bow Street Runners. But the Runners never had a uniform, just a baton bearing a gilt crown which commanded ample respect.

With their glamour and expertise spiced with piratical undertones, the Runners attracted world-wide admiration, not to mention the wrath of a few dignitaries. Charles Dickens wrote: 'There is a vast amount of humbug about these worthies. Apart from many being men of very indifferent character, and far too much in the habit of consorting with thieves and the like, they never lost a public occasion for jobbing and trading in mystery and making the most of themselves.' Indisputably they made the most of themselves – Townsend, the most famous of them, reputedly left £20,000 on his death in 1832, while another, John Sayer, supposedly left £30,000.

Who knows how much Edmund Blackstone left.